PUFFIN

The New C
The Gas-fit

Philip Pullman was born in Norwich in 1946. He was brought up in Africa, Australia, London and Wales, and went to Oxford University to read English. He now lives in Oxford.

Also by Philip Pullman

THE NEW CUT GANG:
THUNDERBOLT'S WAXWORK

Philip Pullman

The New Cut Gang
The
Gas-fitters'
Ball

Illustrated by Mark Thomas

PUFFIN BOOKS

PUFFIN BOOKS

Published by the Penguin Group
Penguin Books Ltd, 80 Strand, London WC2R 0RL, England
Penguin Putnam Inc., 375 Hudson Street, New York, New York 10014, USA
Penguin Books Australia Ltd, 250 Camberwell Road, Camberwell, Victoria 3124, Australia
Penguin Books Canada Ltd, 10 Alcorn Avenue, Toronto, Ontario, Canada M4V 3B2
Penguin Books India (P) Ltd, 11 Community Centre, Panchsheel Park, New Delhi – 110 017, India
Penguin Books (NZ) Ltd, Cnr Rosedale and Airborne Roads, Albany, Auckland, New Zealand
Penguin Books (South Africa) (Pty) Ltd, 24 Sturdee Avenue, Rosebank 2196, South Africa

Penguin Books Ltd, Registered Offices: 80 Strand, London WC2R 0RL, England

www.penguin.com

First published by Viking 1995
Published in Puffin Books 1998
9

Text copyright © Philip Pullman, 1995
Illustrations copyright © Mark Thomas, 1995
All rights reserved

The moral right of the author and illustrator has been asserted

Made and printed in England by Clays Ltd, St Ives plc

British Library Cataloguing in Publication Data
A CIP catalogue record for this book is available from the British Library

ISBN 0–140–36411–0

Contents

One

The Love Phoby

There was a terrible shortage of crime in Lambeth in the summer of 1894, and the New Cut Gang were lamenting the fact, loudly.

'Dunno what's got into 'em,' said eleven-year-old Benny Kaminsky, hurling his penknife for the twentieth time at one of the timbers in the stable-loft, and missing for the nineteenth. 'Seems to me they lost all their gumption, them crooks.'

'Maybe they've reformed,' suggested Thunderbolt Dobney, shoving up his glasses with a dirty forefinger. Thunderbolt was a tender-hearted youth a little younger than Benny, always willing to think the best of anyone. 'They might've given up crime and taken to market-gardening or summing. Like old Dippy gave up picking pockets.'

'He never really picked anyone's pocket,' said Angela Peretti. 'He made out he was a pickpocket to impress people.'

'Only no one was impressed,' pointed out her twin, Zerlina.

The twins were a year or two younger than Benny and Thunderbolt. Being girls, they would normally have had no place in a gang of desperadoes, except that everyone around the New Cut feared them superstitiously. Even Crusher Watkins of the Lower Marsh Gang had a healthy respect for them. They were small for their age, as pretty as angels, and so wicked they were hardly human; they were like a pair of dangerous spirits from the ancient Mediterranean, miraculously reborn in the dusty streets of Lambeth. Better to have them in the gang than out of it, said Benny, and the others could only agree.

Benny scowled and retrieved his penknife from the straw. 'Well, if someone don't do a robbery or a swindle or a murder soon,' he said, 'we might as well give up being detectives altogether. There's no future in it. Might as well take to begging. Might as well starve.'

It was July, and hot heavy weather. Everything was lethargic, from the water in the Metropolitan Drinking Fountain to the sweep of the old horse Jasper's tail, brushing away the sleepy flies in the stable below the New Cut Gang's hideout. And half the gang were off visiting cousins in Ireland or uncles in Manchester; and even the criminal world seemed to have packed its bags and gone on holiday. No crime! It was a dismal prospect.

Benny took aim once more at the post and flicked the knife at it. He was being a Gaucho Knife Artist, like The Amazing Gonzales, whom he and Thunderbolt had seen at the Music Hall the week before. Señor Gonzales (whose name, when Benny pronounced it, rhymed with Wales) had a beautiful assistant called Carmencita, whom he tied to a board and hurled a dozen wicked-looking knives at with stupendous force. When the assistant was untied, there was her outline in knives. Señor Gonzales then repeated the stunt, but blindfold, and with Carmencita spinning around so fast on a revolving board that she seemed to have ten heads and twenty feet.

2

Naturally, this was a trick that Benny could have done just as easily, if he had the knives and the assistant; but with his one flimsy penknife, and with neither of the twins willing to oblige, what could he do?

The world was against him. Moodily he flung the knife, and once again it bounced off and buried itself in the flea-infested straw under the eaves.

'Well, we got Dick to meet Daisy in the park,' said Angela. 'So *that's* summing useful done.'

Thunderbolt and Benny perked up at once. They could win money on this.

'Is he gonna do it?' said Thunderbolt excitedly. 'Is he gonna propose?'

Dick Smith was a young gas-fitter, popular in the New Cut for his prowess as a cricketer, and Daisy Miller was a pretty young woman who everyone agreed would make the ideal bride for Dick. As a matter of fact, Dick thought so too; and so did Daisy.

The trouble was, Dick was too shy to ask her, and this had led the sporting citizens of the New Cut to make several bets on whether he would or not. Snake-Eyes Melmott, the local bookie, started by offering six to four against a marriage, and found some takers at those odds; but Dick couldn't bring himself to propose to her, and Daisy was getting impatient, and soon the price lengthened to two to one. And at those odds, sixpence would win a shilling, and Benny and Thunderbolt found themselves strongly tempted to back Dick to propose, for they had a secret source of information.

And that was the Peretti twins. Angela earned a

shilling or two by helping out at the Smiths', and Zerlina did the same at the Millers', so they had Dick and Daisy well under control.

'They're going to meet in the park?' said Benny. 'When?'

'Six o'clock,' said Zerlina. 'We told 'em to. He's bound to propose soon. He might do it today, if he can get his courage up.'

'How much did you bet with old Snake-Eyes?' said Angela.

'Half a crown,' said Benny.

'I bet a shilling,' said Thunderbolt. 'I wish I'd had a bit more. We can't lose!'

'I reckon we ought to get down the park and encourage him,' said Benny. 'It's – ' He lifted one of the loose tiles and peered through the roof at the clock on the jeweller's opposite. 'It's nearly half-past five now. Come on! Let's go and cheer him on!'

The park was a scruffy patch of grass, muddy in winter and dusty in summer, set about with a few dozen trees, a bandstand, and a pond on which swam a family of depraved and malevolent ducks. Once, when Benny and Thunderbolt and Danny Schneider (currently visiting the uncle in Manchester) had paddled across the water in a tea-chest to the six-foot-square island in the middle, in order to set up camp and live off the wildlife, the ducks had fought them off with such passion that Benny still had a scar on his knee. And then the evil birds had sunk the tea-chest, so the gang had had to wade ashore covered in shame, to the immense amusement of their deadly rivals, the Lower Marsh Gang. Ever since then, Benny had stayed clear of the ducks, and treated all mention of them with disdain.

'Ducks?' he'd say. 'Oh, is there ducks on the pond? I never noticed. I don't think much to ducks.'

Luckily, Dick and Daisy were going to meet on a bench by the bandstand, nowhere near the pond.

'There's a great big bush just behind,' said Angela. 'We could hide in that and whisper to him what to say next.'

'Well, she'd hear as well, wouldn't she?' said Benny. 'She'd think it was a bit funny being proposed to by a talking bush. We better keep out the way. We'll watch from the bandstand, and then when he kisses her we'll go and get his signature on a piece of paper proving he asked her to marry him, and then go straight off and find Snake-Eyes Melmott. Two to one! I'll have seven and sixpence, with me stake money back!'

'I'll have three bob,' said Thunderbolt.

'They *do* kiss 'em, don't they, when they've proposed?' Benny asked, just to be sure.

'Sometimes even before,' said Angela.

'Sometimes more before than afterwards,' added Zerlina.

'Anyway, it'll be easy to tell,' said Benny.

So the gang hung about the bandstand, swinging on the rails, hurling sticks on to the roof, clambering around the outside without their feet touching the ground, and so on, all the time keeping one eye out for the park-keeper and the other on the bench where Dick was going to meet Daisy.

They didn't have long to wait.

Dick, dressed in his off-duty best striped suit and

clutching a wilting bunch of violets in a trembling hand, arrived at the bench at five to six. His warmest admirers wouldn't have called him handsome, but he was a cheerful, friendly, honest-looking chap, and as brave a batsman as ever faced a bouncer; but today he looked pitiful. He kept running his finger around inside his collar, and fanning himself with his straw boater, and biting his fingernails.

'He looks like the prisoner in 'The Primrose Path, or If Only He Had Known', just after they condemned him to death,' said Thunderbolt. 'Me and Pa saw it last week.'

'Sssh!' said Benny. 'There's Daisy, look. I mean *don't* look.'

Daisy Miller was the prettiest young woman in the New Cut: everyone said so. She looked especially fetching on this warm summer evening, in a floral dress and a big hat with cherries on it, and the way her eyes lit up when she saw Dick made the New Cut Gang think that their bets were as good as won.

Little by little the kids stopped what they were doing and shuffled closer to the bench to listen.

'Hello, Dick!' said Daisy. 'Fancy meeting you here.'

'Yeah,' said Dick. 'Imagine that, eh. Ha! Cor.'

'Oh, you got some flowers, Dick! They look half dead.'

'They're for you, Daisy,' he mumbled, and shoved them at her like a saucepan he'd just discovered behind the stove with last month's stew in it.

'Oh, Dick! They're beautiful! I better get 'em in some water, else they'll snuff it,' she said, taking them graciously. 'Shall we – er – shall we sit down, Dick?'

6

He gulped.

'Er – yeah. Might as well, eh,' he said finally.

Daisy sat on the bench, and smiled nicely at Dick. He perched uncomfortably on the very end and stared hard into the middle distance.

By that time the kids were all behind the bush, frankly mesmerized. Benny saw a vision of his seven shillings and sixpence: a fortune, to be spent on ice-creams and ginger snaps for weeks to come. Thunderbolt (a sentimental soul) was looking forward to the kiss. As for the twins, they were burning to defeat Snake-Eyes Melmott; so they were all willing Dick to move closer to Daisy, and above all, *say* something to her. He seemed to be in a trance.

Daisy sat and twiddled the violets. Then she twiddled the cherries on her hat.

'Dick,' she said, and he jumped.

'Er – yeah?'

'You can sit a bit closer, Dick,' she said, and patted the bench.

'Oh. Er . . . Right.'

He moved an inch closer. Then he fanned himself with his hat. Then he took out a handkerchief and mopped his forehead.

'Dick?' said Daisy.

'What?'

'Aren't you going to talk to me?'

He gulped loudly. 'We – er – I – er – ' He ran his fingers around inside his collar again. 'Daisy, I – er – '

'Yes, Dick?'

'I was wondering if – umm – '

'Yes?'

He gulped. 'Daisy, we got a new kind of fitting in

8

today,' he said desperately. 'At the works. A new – umm – fitting.'

'A what?'

'A fitting. A gas fitting. It's called Wilkins' Excelsior New Improved Patent Self-Adjusting Pressure Tap. It's got two kinds of outlets, see, so you can have high-pressure for cooking and low-pressure for lights.'

'Oh,' she said. 'That's nice. But Dick – '

'Yeah,' he said. 'It's ever so good. What you do is, you cut off the mains and get a two-way valve – '

'Dick!'

'– and then you put the rubber seal on the flange, and – '

'*Dick!*'

'What?'

'Do you love me or don't you?'

'*Eh?*'

He goggled at her, pale and sweating. Then he looked around for escape. The kids in the bush were nearly hopping with impatience.

'Say yes!' hissed Angela, and Zerlina clapped her hand over her sister's mouth.

'Cause if you don't,' said Daisy tearfully, 'I can't go on waiting, Dick, I really can't. Cause you know I – I – Cause you know Mr Horspath is – is – Oh, Dick! Honestly!'

And she stamped to her feet and swept away, leaving Dick to scratch his head in helpless despair.

'Who's Mr Horspath?' whispered Thunderbolt.

'He's the Deputy Manger at the Gasworks,' said Zerlina. 'He's courting her, and all.'

Dick, hearing her voice, turned around miserably.

'Wotcher, Dick,' said Angela, clambering out of the bush.

'Wotcher,' said Dick.

'What's up with Daisy?' said Zerlina.

The twins sat on either side of him. Thunderbolt and Benny thought they'd better stay in the bush.

'I dunno,' Dick said. 'I'd like to tell Daisy I love her, and all that sort of thing, and ask her to marry me, but blimey, whenever it comes near the point I get so blooming shy I dunno where to put meself. And now Mr Horspath's courting her as well, I ain't got a hope. I might as well go and drown meself in the duckpond.'

'She wouldn't like you then,' said Angela, thinking of what Benny and the others had looked like after their encounter with the ducks.

'It's not that I'm frightened,' said Dick. 'I'm brave all right. I could fight a lion, or anything. But I'm just too blooming shy . . . And there's the Gas-Fitters' Ball next week. If only I can get her to come to that I know I'll be able to propose, only I'll never get round to it now. I'm a failure. I'm a ruined man. I'm doomed.'

He groaned heavily.

'Why don't you take her to the Music Hall?' said Zerlina.

'D'you think that'd do any good?' he said.

'Yeah!' said Angela. 'Bound to. There's The Amazing Gonzales – he'd put you in the mood. And there's Orlando the Strong Man, and Miss Dolly Walters the Clapham Nightingale. It's a good bill this week.'

'You might be right, kids,' said Dick. 'I suppose

if she was enjoying the show and I asked her sort of casual-like to come to the Ball, I suppose she might.'

'Bound to!'

The twins' confidence was uncanny. There was a great deal about the twins that was uncanny, in Dick's view; like many people, he found them even more disturbing when they were being helpful than when they were intent on mayhem.

'So we'll see Daisy and tell her, then,' said Zerlina. 'You be at the Music Hall tomorrow evening, and she'll be there, and as soon as you've seen The Amazing Gonzales, ask her to come to the Ball.'

'All right!' said Dick. 'I'll do it. Or I might do it after the Clapham Nightingale. Depends.'

'Just make sure you do,' said Angela darkly, and something in the way she said it made Dick think of assassins, and feuds, and bandits with long knives.

'I will, honest,' he gulped.

Thunderbolt and Benny came out of the bush. Dick had wandered away weakly, and the twins had chased off after Daisy.

'I reckon it'll work,' said Benny. 'It can't fail. You know what, we oughter set up training people to do things they're nervous about doing. Like suppose you had a cabman as was nervous of horses – we could train him to like 'em. Or a greengrocer as was frightened of cabbages. We could – '

'Frightened of cabbages?'

'You get all sorts of strange fears,' Benny explained. 'They're called phobies. I heard the itnertist talk about 'em – Dr Psycho – *you* remember. Him as itnertized old Dippy Hitchcock into thinking he was a chicken. You get spider phobies, and horse phobies, and cabbage phobies, and all sorts. Dick's got a love phoby. Anyway – '

'But if a person was frightened of cabbages,' persisted Thunderbolt, 'they wouldn't want to be a greengrocer in the first place.'

'But if they *was*,' said Benny hotly, 'we could train 'em out of it, and then they *could* be one. Seems to me you don't *want* to help Dick. Seems to me you don't *want* to win this bet. You probably got a bet phoby,' he added severely.

Thunderbolt wasn't sure about that. He hadn't bet money very often, because Pa didn't approve except for sixpence on the Derby, but when he had (with the twins' advice) he'd generally been lucky. But then, the twins' advice was usually sound, and they'd advised him to put everything he had on Dick at two to one. It had troubled Thunderbolt a bit, though, because the shilling he'd bet with Snake-Eyes Melmott had actually been given him by Pa to pay for a trigonometry lesson, and if Dick didn't propose soon, Thunderbolt would be in trouble.

Trigonometry was a new craze for Thunderbolt. He'd become interested in it ever since reading about how the great detective Sexton Blake solved a murder mystery by using it to work out precisely what angle the sun had been at in order to shine through the magnifying glass and light the fuse that set off the dynamite attached to the kidnapped Brazilian heiress. Clearly trigonometry was essential in the detective profession, and luckily there lived nearby someone who could teach it to him.

This was Miss Honoria Whittle, the daughter of Mr Horace Whittle, the Chief Manager of the Phoenix Gasworks. Miss Whittle was a nice lady, Thunderbolt thought, and clever too, because she'd been to college and learned to be a teacher. She gave Thunderbolt trigonometry lessons once a week, on Thursdays, which (come to think of it) was today, and if he didn't hurry, he'd be late.

He said goodbye to Benny and raced off to the Whittles' house in Nelson Square, where Miss Whittle was waiting for him as usual in the dining room, with the textbooks all ready. She was a gentle-looking lady, just getting a bit faded, with soft blonde hair and soft blue eyes. She wasn't as pretty as Daisy, of course, but then Miss Whittle was really old, sixty probably, or maybe thirty, anyway.

'Hello, Sam,' she said, because he was only called Thunderbolt on gang business.

'Miss Whittle,' he said, 'd'you reckon someone could have a love phoby?'

'A what?'

'I mean Dick Smith, who's in love with Daisy Miller, only he daren't ask her. Benny reckons he's got a love phoby.'

'Ah! I think you mean phobia. Well, you could be right. I think I knew someone who had a love phobia,' she added.

'Was he in love with you?' said Thunderbolt, interested.

Miss Whittle coughed wistfully. 'Come on, Sam, let's do some work,' she said, and they began.

13

Thunderbolt was half anxious in case she asked him for the shilling, but she was too nice to fuss. When they'd finished the trigonometry, she gave him a biscuit as she always did, and they talked about Dick and Daisy. Miss Whittle was really interested. Thunderbolt was itching to tell her about the bet, because perhaps she might like to put some money on too. But he didn't.

That night one of Benny's wishes came true. He wanted a crime to solve, and someone provided Lambeth with a first-rate one.

The Worshipful Company of Gas-Fitters had several valuable silver dishes and trophies and so on, which they kept in a cabinet in Gas-Fitters' Hall, near the Phoenix Gasworks. There were salt-cellars and soup tureens and goblets and salvers, and the prize of the whole collection was the Jabez Calcutt Memorial Trophy for the apprentice gas-fitter of the year, consisting of a solid silver gas-fitters' wrench mounted on an ebony plinth and surrounded with silver laurel leaves. Dick's name was on it, because he'd won it when he was an apprentice. It was a real work of art.

And that night someone broke into Gas-Fitters' Hall and stole the lot.

Two

The Swedish Lucifer

The news of the burglary was all round the New Cut before breakfast. Ordinary burglaries were one thing, but this was a bigger job altogether than pinching a sack of potatoes from the greengrocer's or a tin alarm clock from the pawnbroker's window. The Worshipful Company of Gas-Fitters was an important body of men, and Gas-Fitters' Hall was the most noble edifice in the whole of Lambeth, apart from the Archbishop's Palace and the Lunatic Asylum, anyway.

As soon as the kids heard about it they ran there at once, and found a crowd gathered outside, staring at four policemen who were pretending to look for clues.

'I hear as they drugged the night-watchman,' said Dippy Hitchcock, the hot-chestnut and baked-potato man. 'They slipped him an unknown Chinese poison in a cup of tea, and he fell asleep and never heard nothing.'

Benny and the others listened, enthralled.

'I don't know about that,' said Mr Myhill solemnly, 'but I'm given to understand that that silver's worth over ten thousand pounds.'

Mr Myhill was a bank clerk, and understood the value of money.

'Daft, if you ask me,' said Mrs Fanny Blodgett of the Excelsior Tea and Coffee Rooms. 'What do a lot of blooming gas-fitters want with ten thousand quid's worth of silver plate?'

The men turned to her, shocked.

'Mrs Blodgett!' said Mr Tate the pawnbroker. 'The Worshipful Company of Gas-Fitters is a most ancient and honourable charitable association, fit to rank with the Dyers, the Tanners, the Vintners, the Merchant Taylors, all the most noble City Livery companies. Of course they need silver plate. I'm surprised at you for thinking otherwise. I thought you was a woman of sense.'

Benny led the others away urgently down a little alley at the side of the building.

'This is the crime we been waiting for!' he said. 'I bet we can solve it. I bet the police can't. I bet Scotland Yard's baffled. I reckon it's an inter-national gang, that's what I reckon.'

'Or pirates!' said Angela. 'Off a boat on the river. Bound to be.'

'I just hope we can solve it before Sexton Blake gets to hear about it,' said Thunderbolt.

'Well come on!' said Benny. 'What we waiting for?'

'Look at this,' said Thunderbolt. 'Here's a clue straight off.'

He pointed down at the ground. Because of the dry weather, there wasn't much mud about just then, but a leaking overflow pipe somewhere above had dripped on to the dust in the alley and created a churned-up patch of wet yellowish earth.

'If we find someone with that colour mud on their boots,' Thunderbolt said, 'they're as good as guilty. Sexton Blake knows all the different colours of

London mud. He's always checking boots and that. We oughter do the same.'

'And footprints,' said Angela. 'We could look for footprints in it.'

'Yeah!' said Thunderbolt. 'That's a good idea.'

'That's what I mean,' said Angela. 'And we could of, and all, till you put your great plates all over it.'

Thunderbolt looked down. She was right; he'd trodden everything into a swamp. If there'd been any burglarious footprints a moment ago, there were certainly none now.

'H'mm,' he said. 'Oh well.'

Benny was peering closely at a little window four feet above the ground.

'Here's a clue,' he said.

The others gathered round. Benny was pointing at a dent in the woodwork near the window-catch which looked as if it had been made by a jemmy.

'That's where they forced their way in!' said Benny. 'Betcher!'

'Yeah, could be!' said Zerlina.

Thunderbolt was peering at it closely. His glasses didn't always work when he hadn't cleaned them for a while, and it was hard to clean them anyway given the usual state of his handkerchief, so he couldn't see the little dent as well as the others could. He felt along the window-sill and found something else, though.

'Here's a drop of wax, look.'

The others demanded to feel it too. It was almost invisible, but their fingers could make it out all right.

'A little blob of wax,' said Benny. 'That's *definitely*

17

a clue! He musta spilled it from a candle. And look –
here's a lucifer!'

He had spotted a match lying at the foot of the
wall, and stooped to pick it up. This was the real
thing, and no error. A genuine criminal match, com-
bined with a genuine criminal blob of candle-wax
right next to a genuine criminal jemmy-dent – it was
too good to be true.

'OY!'

The roar resounded down the alley, and all the
kids looked up, startled. P.C. Jellicoe, the stoutest
policeman in the whole of Lambeth, was standing in
the entrance.

'Get out of it! Go on! Move along there!'

Benny darted up to him, holding the match.

'Mr Jellicoe! Look what we found! It's a clue!'

'Oh, it's you lot,' said P.C. Jellicoe, recognizing
him. 'Go on, hop it. This is a serious police investi-
gation. What you doing here anyway? You oughter
be in school. Or prison. I know where I'd send
yer.'

'But Mr Jellicoe – '

'Did you hear what I said? Clear off!'

'But we got a – '

P.C. Jellicoe's mighty hand, raised high, showed
them clearly what they'd get if they didn't do as he
said. They dodged past him out of the alley and
stopped in the street to look back.

'No good telling old Jelly-Belly,' said Benny. 'It's
the Inspector we ought to tell. He'll know about
clues and that.'

But the Inspector was inside the building, and the
constable on guard at the door was even less patient

than P.C. Jellicoe. Benny had to move fast to dodge the automatic clout.

'Right,' he said hotly to the policeman. 'That's it. You done it now. When the New Cut Gang catches the burgular as done this job, you're going to look pretty silly. I wouldn't like to be in your boots. I wouldn't like to be a policeman then. I'd rather be a pantomime horse than a policeman when we catch the Gas-Fitters' Hall burgular.'

The policeman sneered, and Benny and the others left in disdain.

'You better not lose that match,' said Angela. 'Give us it here, I'll look after it.'

'Not blooming likely,' said Benny. 'Remember when you looked after Sharky Bob for the afternoon?'

Sharky Bob was the youngest member of the New Cut Gang, a cheerful, benevolent six-year-old who would eat anything, and often did. The twins had once borrowed him for an afternoon in order to match him against The Brixton Gobbler, an infant of similar talents, in a contest involving hard-boiled eggs. Sharky had beaten The Gobbler hands down, and the twins, who had bet a total of nine shillings on him, had run off at once to claim their winnings from Snake-Eyes Melmott. In doing so they'd forgotten Sharky Bob altogether. He was later found happily eating his way up the Lambeth Walk from chop-house to pub to baked-potato stall, followed by an admiring crowd, but the damage had been done: the twins had earned a reputation. They won bets, but they lost things.

They gave Benny a dark look, but he was intent

on fumbling in his pocket for something to put the match in.

'Here it is,' he said. 'I'll keep it in me matchbox.'

He brought out a Bryant and May's matchbox and carefully slid it open. He had to be careful in case the unusual worm he kept in there had come alive again, but it was either dead or asleep. The worm was unknown to science, Thunderbolt said, but then, after three weeks in Benny's pocket, probably not even its mother would have known it.

Benny prodded the worm carefully aside and put the match in the box. Or tried to.

'Here,' he said, 'it won't go.'

The match was too long for the box.

'I thought all matches was the same?' said Zerlina.

'Give us a look,' said Thunderbolt.

He held it close to his eyes. It looked like every other match he'd ever seen, except that it was, now he looked at it, a bit longer than most.

'This is an even better clue!' he said. 'A highly unusual match!'

'Yeah!' Benny said, excited. 'That's right! Let's go and ask Mr MacPhail about it. He'll know all right.'

MacPhail's was the tobacconist's at the corner of the New Cut. Mr MacPhail sold snuff and walking-sticks and Smokers' Companions as well as tobacco and cigars and cigarettes and things, so he was bound to know about matches.

'Aye,' he said, examining it through his pince-nez. 'Swedish, this is. Not a British lucifer. Swedish.'

'How d'you know that, Mr MacPhail?' said Benny. 'I mean, apart from it being long, and that.'

'Because o' these little marks at the end.'

They all crowded round to look. He was pointing at the unburnt end. Thunderbolt, blinking and widening his eyes, could just see two little grooves pressed into the wood on opposite sides of the square stick a fraction of an inch from the end.

'When they make 'em,' Mr MacPhail explained, 'there's a machine that holds the stick by one end and dips it into a tank of thick inflammable stuff. Then they pull it out again with a wee blob on, and that's the head, ye see, and they march the sticks aroond till the head's dry and then pack 'em in the boxes. A British lucifer's made the same way, only British lucifers is held by a different kind o' machine that makes a different kind o' mark. Look.'

He took a Bryant and May's matchbox from the shelf behind him and showed them a match. He was right: on this one, each of the four edges where the sides of the match met had been nipped in a little about an eighth of an inch from the end. It was quite different from the Swedish one.

'D'you sell Swedish matches, Mr MacPhail?' said Thunderbolt.

'No, son. Only British ones.'

'So who d'you reckon might be using Swedish lucifers round here?' said Benny.

'A sailor,' said Mr MacPhail. 'Someone in the timber trade, mebbe. Anyone who's been to the Baltic recently.'

'Or any real Swedes,' said Thunderbolt. 'Like S – '

Benny kicked his ankle to shut him up. 'Right. Thanks, Mr MacPhail,' he said, and they left.

22

Outside in the street, Thunderbolt rubbed his ankle and said 'What was that for?'

'Cause you might warn him, you clot!'

'Warn who? Mr MacPhail's not the burglar, is he?'

'Warn Sid the Swede, of course! That's who you were going to say, wasn't it?'

'Well, yeah,' Thunderbolt admitted.

Sid the Swede was a local villain. He was a furtive and rat-like little man who always seemed to know where you could find a bit of mislaid fruit and veg, or someone who could change the markings on a horse to make it look as if it wasn't the one that was pinched from the stables last week.

'Betcher it ain't Sid the Swede,' said Angela.

'Yeah, me too,' said Zerlina. 'I betcher lots.'

'Give you ten to one,' said Angela.

You didn't bet against the twins, even at odds like that.

'Why not?' said Benny.

'Cause he's in chokey,' said Zerlina, 'that's why. He got caught last week nicking washing off old Mrs Pearson's line.'

'He got jugged for a month,' said Angela.

'H'mm,' said Benny. 'Well, that puts a different confection on things. Seems to me we'll have to go inspecting every blooming box of matches in Lambeth. Every time someone lights a cigar we'll have to pick up the match afterwards and see if it's Swedish.'

'And if they've got yellow mud on their boots,' said Thunderbolt, 'they're done for.'

So the gang split up to go looking for Swedish

matches, yellow mud, and ten thousand pounds worth of silver.

That evening, Dick was going to take Daisy to the Music Hall. The twins wanted to go along too, in order to supervise him, but their mother wouldn't hear of it. She looked up from the table where she was rolling out some pasta and her dark eyes flashed.

'What you tink a you do with that poor boy?' she said. 'You leave him alone! He's a nervous, he's a shy, he don't a want silly faces talking at him to a do this and a say that and all so on. You a pester him, I cut a your troats.'

She reached for the knife with a beefy flour-covered arm, and they fled. Mrs Peretti had been threatening to cut her daughters' throats ever since they could remember. It was just a sign of how fond she was of them, and they always liked to hear it, because it reassured them that everything was all right; but it meant that they'd have to give Dick some careful instructions if he was to face Daisy alone.

They guessed he'd be a little early, so they waylaid him outside the Music Hall three-quarters of an hour before the show began. He was walking up and down the pavement in the sunny evening chewing his nails and muttering to himself.

'What can I do, kids?' he said miserably. 'Look at me! I'm a shadow of a man! I wish Daisy was a heavyweight boxer, and I was going to go three rounds with her. I wouldn't be half so blooming nervous. If only I could think of what to say . . .'

'That's what we've come for, you great goopus,'

said Zerlina. 'Just listen and we'll tell you what to do.'

'Now what ladies like,' said Angela knowledgeably, 'is flattery. You gotta tell her that her eyes is like stars.'

'And her lips is like cherries,' added Zerlina.

'Cherries? You sure?' said Dick.

'That's right. And altogether she looks like a fashion plate.'

'What's a fashion plate?'

The twins weren't sure themselves, but they had an answer; they had an answer for everything.

'It's a special ladies' thing,' said Angela. 'That'll please her, you watch. Then in the interval you buy her an orange.'

'And in the second half you whisper, "Daisy, will you do me the honour of being my guest at the Gas-Fitters' Ball?"'

'And she'll say, "Oh, blimey, Dick, not half."'

'And you say, "Cor, Daisy, I love yer," and –'

'Here she is!'

The twins fled before Daisy could see them. They were like little demons, thought Dick nervously; one second they were here, whispering mischief, the next they'd vanished. And here was Daisy, looking prettier than ever.

'Hello, Dick,' she said sweetly.

He gulped so hard he nearly swallowed his own head.

'Hello, Daisy,' he croaked.

Should he start flattering her straight away? Or should they get inside first? Luckily, the queue was moving forward, and he didn't have time to say anything until he'd bought the tickets and they were sitting in the middle of the stalls. He helped her in and sat down beside her. The band was tuning up in the orchestra pit, the stage curtain was glowing crimson in the limelight, the gilt on the plasterwork was glittering, the boxes and the balcony were all full of jolly-looking people laughing and chattering. Dick looked around desperately, but there was nothing for it; he'd have to talk to her.

What on earth had the twins told him to say? It had gone right out of his head.

'Er – ' he began.

'Yes, Dick?'

'Er – you look like a bowl,' he said.

'What?'

'I mean a plate.'

'A *plate?*'

'Yeah. Or a dish. I mean – '

What Daisy might have said in reply he never knew, because the band struck up with 'Down at the Old Bull and Bush', and she turned away bewildered, to look at the stage as the curtain rose.

During the first half of the bill, they watched Mr Hosmer Simpkins, the Lyrical Tenor; Madame Taroczy's Hungarian Spiral Bicycle Ascensionists; Mr Paddy O'Flynn, the Jolly Wee Man from the Emerald Isle; and the Louisiana Banjo Playboys. In between each act, Dick turned to Daisy and began to speak, but the chairman always spoke louder, and the audience roared with laughter at his jokes, and Dick had to open and shut his mouth like a fish.

At last there came the interval.

'I liked the Spiral Hungarians, Dick,' she said. 'Didn't you?'

'Yeah, I did, yeah,' he agreed. 'Cor. Here, Daisy . . .'

'Yes, Dick?'

'Umm – ' he began. He was trying to remember the other things the twins had told him to say. Wasn't there something to do with the night and the sky? 'Your face,' he said nervously.

'Is there something on it?'

'It's like the – the moon.'

'The *moon*?'

'No, no – that wasn't it. Umm – '

People in the row behind were listening, and enjoying it all immensely. Dick mopped his forehead with a red spotted handkerchief. Perhaps he should have gone back to saying she was like a bowl, only that hadn't come out right, either. But the word bowl made him think of cherries, and then he remembered.

'Umm – your eyes is like cherries, Daisy.'

'What d'you mean, Dick? Are they bloodshot or something?'

'No,' he said. 'No. Not at all. No. What I mean is, your lips. That's what I meant. Like – umm – ' This was awful, he thought. He'd forgotten it altogether, but he had to go on now he'd started. Fruit; some kind of fruit; come *on* . . . Oranges, was it? No; couldn't have been. 'Bananas,' he said desperately.

'Why?' she demanded.

He hadn't the faintest idea.

'Er – same shape,' he mumbled doubtfully.

'What *do* you mean?' she said. 'Honestly, Dick, if I didn't know you better, I'd say you was trying to upset me.'

'Oh, Lor – no – I'm not, honest – '

The people behind were laughing and nudging each other and telling the people in the next row back. More and more of the audience were trying to listen, craning over from the balcony above, peering at them through opera-glasses.

Someone up in the seats behind yelled, 'Go it, Dick! I got five bob on yer!'

Dick looked round, puzzled, because he hadn't the faintest idea what the man meant, of course. Someone else took up the cry, and soon the whole audience was cheering like a racehorse crowd. As for Daisy, she was mortified, poor girl.

'I can't sit here and be laughed at, Dick, I really can't!' she said. 'It's awful! It's just too embarrassing for words! Everybody's listening, and I'm sure you mean well, but – '

And she stood up and struggled to get out along the crowded row of seats. A big groan of disappointment went up. Dick struggled after her, but he was too late; and then the band struck up for the second half of the bill, and the lights went down, and she was gone.

Meanwhile, the twins were pestering their big brother Alfredo to look out for Swedish matches, as the gang were doing. Alf was a hokey-pokey man, an ice-cream vendor, and naturally, spending his time in commerce, he was bound to meet a lot of men who smoked and dropped the matches in the street. So the twins said, anyway.

'D'you mean every time I see some bloke light up a gasper I got to get down on me hands and knees and pick up his dead lucifer? Get out of it!'

He was combing his thick black moustache and smoothing down his glossy black hair in the kitchen mirror, and he was dressed up to the nines.

'Where you going, Alf?' said Zerlina.

'I'm off to see my mate Orlando down the Music Hall. I got a special pass to go in the Stage Door.'

'Orlando the Strong Man?' said Angela.

'Yeah. He bought five pound of ice-cream off me the other day and swallered it just like that. He's a real gentleman. He's the strongest man in the world, I shouldn't wonder.'

'Can we come with yer?'

'Don't see why not, as long as you come straight back.'

So the twins set off with Alf, hoping they might be able to find out how Dick was getting on. They liked going about with their big brother; he was smart and handsome and all the young ladies liked his flashing eyes and his jet-black whiskers, and he was usually good for a lump of hokey-pokey on a hot day, especially if he'd won a bet. He once bet Stan Garside the butcher a whole guinea at a hundred to eight that the Archbishop of Canterbury would come and judge the Elephant and Castle Cat Show. Naturally, Stan thought he was on a winner, but sure enough, His Grace the Lord Archbishop did turn up, and he was as nice as pie. It was the twins who'd done it. They'd just gone to Lambeth Palace, knocked on the door, and asked. When they wanted to be, they were irresistible – or supernatural, one or the other. Anyway, they got a lot of hokey-pokey that day.

They reached the Stage Door and Alf waved his

pass at the old porter, who didn't even look up from his copy of 'Wild West Yarns', and then they were inside the theatre itself.

It was a dark, busy place, smelling of glue and greasepaint, with music and bursts of loud laughter coming from somewhere else in the building. Performers in costumes were waiting in the corridors or coming out of dressing-rooms, a group of stage-carpenters were sitting around a packing-case playing cards, and they all greeted Alf like an old friend.

In one corner of the wings, Orlando the Strong Man was warming up. He was wearing a leopard-skin costume that showed off his mighty muscles, and he had a gleaming bald head and a huge black moustache even bigger than Alf's.

'Wotcher, Alf,' he said, 'and who's these young ladies?'

'Me sisters,' said Alf. 'They come to say hello.'

While Alf went to talk to some of the chorus-girls nearby, Orlando bent down and very politely offered his forefinger to the twins to shake. His hands were too big to shake all at once. As Alf had said, he was a real gentleman.

'Are you the strongest man in the world, Mr Orlando?' said Angela.

'Probably,' he said. 'You seen the act, have yer?'

'Yeah!' said Zerlina. 'We liked the cannon-ball bit best.'

'Ah,' he said. 'That takes practice. You have to –'

But he couldn't say any more because, to everyone's surprise, the curtain nearby swirled open and suddenly there was Daisy. She looked as if she'd been crying.

'Daisy!' said Zerlina.

'What's the matter?' said Angela.

'I – I got lost,' Daisy sniffed. 'I was trying to find me way out and – and –'

'Excuse me, miss,' said Orlando, 'but you seem to be distressed. Can I help in any way?'

'That's very kind of you, Mr . . .'

'This is Orlando,' said Angela. 'He's showing us his muscles.'

'He's got ever such a lot,' said Zerlina.

'Cor,' said Orlando, 'you ain't wrong. Here – look at this.' He struck a pose and flexed his mighty arms. 'You see that muscle there?' he went on, frowning at a spot behind his shoulder.

'Which one?' said Daisy. 'There's hundreds.'

'That one going in and out.'

'There it is!' said Zerlina, pointing.

'Oh yes! I see it now,' said Daisy.

'Well,' said Orlando, 'most people ain't got one of them.'

'Oh,' said Daisy, impressed. 'What does it do?'

'Well, it goes in and out,' said Orlando. 'Here! Did you know I can lift a full-grown ox in my teeth?'

'No! Really?'

'Yeah. The trick is to get it right between the shoulder-blades. You probably wouldn't be able to do it at first. I should practise on a dog if I was you, and work up to a calf. You seen the act?'

Daisy shook her head and dabbed her eyes with a little handkerchief.

'I was going to,' she said, 'but I had to leave.'

'The best bit is where they bounce fifteen

cannon-balls off me head, one after the other. The trick is to get 'em right there,' he added, pointing at the middle of his gleaming forehead, 'else it could be dangerous. Anyway, miss,' he said politely, 'I got to go now, cause I'm on in a minute. I'm very glad to have made your acquaintance.'

He held out his hand, but as she was about to shake it, he took it back.

'No,' he said, 'I better not shake your hand. Shall I tell you why?'

Daisy nodded, surprised.

'Cause this hand can crush rocks,' he said. 'I got to be careful what I do with it. Goodbye, miss, and cheer up, eh?'

Then there was a roll of drums, and he sprang on to the stage to a great round of applause. The twins would have liked to watch, but there was Daisy to look after; things didn't seem to be going very well for the great bet. They took her out and tried to find out what had happened.

Oddly enough, Benny and Thunderbolt were doing the same thing at that very moment, with Dick. He had tried to follow her out of the Music Hall, but had taken a different turning, and run into the boys outside the foyer. They were hanging about watching every smoker with grim suspicion. Every time a match fell to the ground they pounced, but so far they hadn't had any luck.

'You seen Daisy?' Dick said.

'I thought she was with you,' said Benny. 'Here! Thunderbolt! Geezer in the straw hat . . .'

Thunderbolt darted across the road and practically snatched the match out of the hands of a stout man who'd just lit a cigar. He looked at the match closely and shook his head in disappointment. Benny sighed.

'Woss going on?' said Dick.

'We're looking for Swedish matches,' said Benny.

'Oh,' said Dick. Probably collecting them, he thought, like stamps or something. He sighed even more deeply than Benny.

That reminded Benny of the bet, and with an effort he pulled his mind back to it.

'Here,' he said, 'I thought you was going to ask Daisy to the Ball?'

'I was,' said Dick in tones of the deepest gloom. 'But it seems to me that every time I open my mouth, I say the wrong thing. I told her her face was like a bowl of bananas. At least that's what I think I said. I can't remember. It's all gone dark in me mind.'

'H'mm,' said Benny. He didn't know much about the language of love, but he didn't think that sounded like a compliment.

Thunderbolt darted back across the street.

'No good,' he said. 'It was a Bryant and May's. What's the matter with Dick?'

Benny told him. Thunderbolt whistled. 'A bowl of bananas?' he said, impressed. 'Cor. She ought to be pleased, anyway. Anybody'd be flattered by that.'

'You think so?' said Dick, cheering up a little. Maybe it hadn't been such a mistake after all. 'Here, them Swedish matches you're looking for . . .'

'Yeah?' said Benny eagerly.

'Well, I know who'd probably have some. I mean,

being as he went to the European Congress of Gas and Coke Industries in Stockholm last month to make a speech.'

'Who?'

'Mr Whittle,' said Dick. 'I dunno what's bin up with him lately, neither. He's bin acting most peculiar. Almost as if he had summing on his mind. Still, I can't hang about here. I better go and look for Daisy.'

He kicked at a gloomy bit of straw on the pavement and wandered away, sighing. The boys looked at each other with bright speculation in their eyes.

'Mr Whittle . . .' said Benny. 'I wonder.'

'And – and Miss Honoria Whittle was unhappy when I went for me trigonometry lesson. She kept sighing and gazing out the window. I thought she was sad about me not giving her that shilling I bet Snakes-Eyes Melmott, but maybe she was worried about her Pa. Same as I was about my Pa over the snide coins buisness. So maybe he *is* up to summing. Cor!'

'Well,' said Benny, 'there's only one way to find out. We'll have to detect him good and proper. Come on! Let's get going!'

When the twins heard what Dick had said to Daisy, they thought it would be a good idea to keep out of his way for a day or so, in case he thought it was their fault. They knew that other people sometimes found it hard to believe in their good intentions.

'We oughter wrote it down for the great clot to read,' said Angela.

'That'd look good, wouldn't it?' said Zerlina. 'Fish-

34

ing out a bit of paper and reading to her. I dunno what we can do.'

'You can't help some people,' said Angela.

Shaking their heads over the futility of human endeavour, they went home. They were so preoccupied that they didn't see Daisy, at her front door, being stopped by a handsome young man with fair curly hair, who lifted his hat very politely and told her how pretty she was looking. The young man was Mr Horspath, the Deputy Gasworks Manager, Daisy's other admirer. It was lucky for him the twins weren't watching, or they'd have been there in a second, to get him away from Daisy at all costs. Snake-Eyes Melmott was taking a lot of money in bets on him, and Daisy's mother strongly approved of Mr Horspath, because he had nice soft hands, she said, like a proper gentleman, not great rough oily shovels like Dick's. There was no doubt about it, Mr Horspath was a serious threat.

Three

The Albatross-loft

There were some things that Benny had to do alone. He trusted Thunderbolt completely, but trying to make Thunderbolt less clumsy was like teaching a horse to knit, and this job needed care. As for the twins – he shuddered at the thought.

Anyway, the great detective Sexton Blake didn't always take Tinker his boy assistant everywhere he went. Benny read about Sexton Blake's adventures every week in the *Halfpenny Marvel*, and he didn't have a high opinion of Tinker. Tinker's main duties seemed to consist of running about with messages, of handing Sexton Blake his magnifying glass, and of getting hit over the head by crooks, and Benny regarded him with patronizing scorn. Tinker couldn't have solved the snide coin mystery, could he? The New Cut Gang had wrapped that up triumphantly.

No, in Benny's eyes, he was the boss, and the rest of the gang went where he led and did as he told them; though he kept his fingers crossed superstitiously in the case of the twins. There had been many occasions on which Benny had been tempted to jump on an omnibus and travel across the river to Baker Street, knock on the great detective's door, and ask his opinion, as one professional to another. And this was one. Unfortunately, according to the current edition of the *Halfpenny Marvel*, Mr Blake was at the moment chained up in the cellar of an evil slave-trader in Constantinople, with a bottle of acid eating its way through the rope holding shut a cage of half-starved, plague-bearing rats. Benny reckoned the great detective had his hands full for the moment, though no doubt he'd be free next week.

So he sat through supper that evening fuming with impatience. Cousin Morris had looked in, as he often did, and he and Benny's father sat at the table as the late evening sunlight slanted through the parlour window, arguing at enormous length about whether or not the late Duke of Clarence had been a good or a bad influence on gentlemen's fashion. They could never agree on anything, Pa and Cousin Morris. Then Mr Schneider from next door came to join in the discussion, and Benny's mother and his elder sister Leah made sarcastic remarks about the vanity and fussiness of men compared to the restraint and modesty of women.

Benny got up at one point and said, 'Excuse me, but I got summing important to do –' and his father said 'No! No! Sit down! It'll do you good to hear a proper intelligent debate!'

And Cousin Morris said, 'Benny, Benny! This is golden wisdom we're talking here! There's people as would pay money to hear the quality of argument you get at your father's table! Isn't that right, Mr Schneider?'

'There's plenty in Parliament as could wish for the eloquence and fluency what runs as freely and nourishingly here as Mrs Kaminsky's chicken soup,' said Mr Schneider gallantly.

Benny's mother, clearing the table, rolled her eyes at Leah and said nothing. Benny sat where he was until they allowed him to go, and then raced up to his room in the attic, where he got down to some proper detecting.

He thought that Sexton Blake would want another look at the match first, so he fished it out of the folded bit of paper in which he kept it for safety and scrutinized it fiercely through his grubby magnifying-glass.

The head was only just burned, which meant that the match had been struck to light it and blown out almost at once. You could light a cigarette like that, or a lantern, but not a cigar; they took longer. Some of the wood below the head would have been burnt away as well. That was worth knowing, thought Benny.

What would Sexton Blake do once he'd found that out? Make a note of it, probably. Benny tore a page out of the back of his History exercise book and wrote:

Clue number 1.
Sweedish match. Probly used for lighthing cigrette or candel.

Then he remembered something else, and wrote:

Clue number 2.
Blob of wax on winder sill of burguled premmiss's. Probly from a candel.

In a frenzy of enthusiasm he went on:

38

Clue number 3.
Dent like what a jemmy would make next to winder.

He thought about the yellow mud, but that wasn't a clue in itself. It would only be a clue if he saw some on someone's boots. Finally he wrote:

Clue number 4.
Mr Whittle has been in Sweeden.

·That made him wonder what Sexton Blake would do about Mr Whittle. What he'd probably do, Benny thought, was disguise himself, and watch him like a hawk. The criminal always returned to the scene of the crime – everyone knew that. So if Benny saw Mr Whittle slinking back guiltily to Gas-Fitters' Hall, he was as good as caught.

The trouble was . . .

The trouble was, Mr Whittle was a nice man. He always shelled out generously when Guy Fawkes' Day came round; he'd seen the New Cut Gang once playing a game of street cricket against the Lower Marsh mob, during one of their rare truces, and he'd rolled his sleeves up and joined in, bowling out Crusher Watkins with a cunning off-break; and he always had his suits made at Kaminsky's, despite being rich enough, said Benny's father, to go to Savile Row.

However, a detective's duty was to detect, and Benny couldn't shirk it. As soon as school was out next day, he told Thunderbolt what he was going to do, and gave him solemn instructions about the future of the gang if he didn't come back.

Thunderbolt gaped. 'D'you mean – '

'What I mean is, this is a secret and dangerous enterprise what could easily go wrong,' said Benny grimly. 'He could be the head of an international gang of desperate robbers. He could've been acting the manager of the gasworks just in order to lull everyone's suspicions. I bet he's just carrying on acting it for the time being till everyone forgets about the robbery, and then he'll be off to Monte Carlo to spend the money. Like as not Miss Whittle ain't his daughter either.'

'I think she is,' said Thunderbolt doubtfully.

'I bet she's really called Diamond Lou or Six-Gun Betsy. She probably done the robbery with him. She's probably got one of them little guns in her stocking, a derringer, like Madame Carlotta had in the last Sexton Blake. She's probably waiting for you to make a trigonometry mistake and she'll plug you. I bet she's killed half a dozen –'

Thunderbolt knew the signs; this was where one of Benny's fantasies was leaving the ground.

'But what you gonna *do*?' he interrupted.

'Foller him everywhere,' said Benny. 'Like a shadder. He won't know I'm there, cause I'll be in disguise. You watch.'

Benny's idea of disguise was a comprehensive one. Finding clothes wasn't too difficult, because his father's workshop was usually full of suits waiting to be altered or paid for. He'd managed to borrow a smallish one in a vivid check, which had been waiting six months for its owner to come out of prison,

and which he was sure wouldn't be missed. It only needed the trousers rolling up nine inches or so and the jacket padding out with newspaper. The sleeves were a bit long, but he could always pretend to have lost both hands in a fight with a shark. To go with the suit he had borrowed a brown bowler hat from his sister Leah's young man Joe.

Once the suit was on, he set about colouring his hair grey with a handful of flour, painting on a vast and sooty moustache with a burnt cork, and giving himself a hideous bright red scar from forehead to jaw. He turned his face this way and that in the broken little bit of mirror they had in the hideout, and which they normally used as a periscope, when it wasn't being a heliograph. He couldn't speak; he was lost in admiration.

'What's the matter?' said Thunderbolt after a minute. 'It's not so bad. You just need to – '

'You know what,' said Benny suddenly, 'I oughter go on the stage.'

'Like Four-Ball?'

Danny Schneider, the gang member who'd been condemned to a month in Manchester, was known as Four-Ball because of his juggling skills. There was no doubt that he'd be topping the bill at the Music Hall one day, but that wasn't what Benny had meant.

'No,' he said. 'Like Henry Irving. They oughter do a play about Sexton Blake, and I could play him. And then when he was tied up in a cellar or summing I could play Dr Skull, the mad scientist. Then when Dr Skull gets killed by one of the evil ape-men I could play a good ape-man and rescue Sexton Blake, and then I could play him again. And then —'

'But what are you going to do about Mr Whittle?'

With a mighty effort Benny frowned, shook his head, and brought himself back to the present.

'Eh? Oh, him. I'll just foller him after he leaves the gasworks. He's bound to return to the scene of the crime, cause they always do. Then when I see him do that, I'll make a citizen's arrest.'

Thunderbolt opened his mouth to point out that Mr Whittle was a leading member of the Board of the Worshipful Company of Gas-Fitters, and he was bound to be visiting Gas-Fitters' Hall before long anyway; but you couldn't argue with Benny, somehow. Thunderbolt watched his leader saunter off in his voluminous check suit, hitching up the trousers for the tenth time in twenty paces, pushing up the bowler hat from the bridge of his nose, a drift of flour trailing behind him, and felt nothing but honest admiration.

Dick came out of work in a savage mood. He'd been feeling cross all day, and late that afternoon he wrenched so hard at a Wilkins' Excelsior New Improved Patent Self-Adjusting Pressure Tap that he broke the flange and had to pay for a replacement, which didn't improve his temper one bit.

So when Angela and Zerlina saw him coming, they were glad they were in the company of their new friend, The Mighty Orlando. He was off duty, so he wasn't wearing his leopard-skin; he was looking very smart in a striped blazer and a Panama hat. He had stopped at Alf's ice-cream stall for a refreshing gallon of strawberry-and-vanilla, and the twins had been hanging about there too, and Orlando had kindly bought them a lump each; and they were strolling along together past the gasworks in the

43

sunshine when Dick came out with a face like thunder. Orlando was big enough for both the twins to hide behind him, but they were too late.

'Wotcher, gals,' Dick said gloomily.

They looked at each other quickly. Perhaps he wasn't cross with them after all.

'Wotcher, Dick,' said Angela. 'This is The Mighty Orlando.'

'He's a friend of ours,' said Zerlina meaningfully.

'And this is Mister Dick Smith,' said Angela to Orlando.

'How d'you do, mate,' said Dick, holding out his hand.

'Pleased to meet yer,' said Orlando. 'No – I won't shake your hand. Shall I tell you why?'

'Yeah, go on,' said Dick.

'Cause this hand can crush rocks,' said Orlando solemnly, pointing to his right hand with a left forefinger the size of a cricket-bat handle. 'Find a rock – go on. Any rock. I'll show yer.'

'No, I believe yer,' said Dick, impressed. 'Cor.'

Feeling a little safer now, the twins told Dick about meeting Daisy in the Music Hall the night before. Dick looked embarrassed.

'Yeah,' he said. 'I spose I must've got it wrong, all them things you told me to say. I spose Daisy'll never want to see me again. I spose Mr Horspath'll have her all to hisself from now on.'

And he sighed like a 'Thunderer' Pneumatic Drainage Pump, and sat down wearily on the edge of the nearest horse-trough.

'I knows how yer feel,' said Orlando. 'Mind if I join yer?'

Dick moved up to make room. 'You had love trouble as well, mate?' he said.

'Not half,' said Orlando.

The twins perched on the horse-trough and listened, enthralled.

Orlando fanned himself with his hat, and went on: 'Oh, yus. I was in love and all, same as you, only I could never work up the nerve to tell her. I done all kinds of things to please her, like tearing books in half and crushing rocks and bouncing cannon-balls off me head, but I could never come out with saying I loved her.'

'That's just the same as me!' said Dick.

'And by the time I found out what to do, it was too late. Fate had passed me by.'

'You mean you *did* find out what to do?'

'Oh, yus. I know what to do now all right. Only like I say, it's too late.'

'So what is it? What's the secret?'

'The secret of love,' said Orlando, 'was told to me by a Spanish hacrobat in a circus what I worked in once. And he oughter known, cause he had six wives at least. In different countries, of course. What he said was, you take a deep breath, close your eyes, grab hold of her hand, and cover it with burning kisses. About a dozen, he said. Once you done that, you feel quite different. Telling her you love her's easy after that.'

'And have you tried it?'

'No, I ain't,' said Orlando, 'cause of my undying love for the lady what I never done it to in the first place.'

Dick was nodding. There was a strange light in his eyes.

'Take a deep breath –' he repeated.

'That's it.'

'Close me eyes – '

'Yus.'

'Grab her hand – '

'That's the style.'

'And cover it with burning kisses.'

'About a dozen,' said the twins together.

'And if you do that,' said Orlando, 'I guarantee you'll be able to ask her to marry yer, and she won't have no choice but to say yes, because she'll be bowled over by your passion. Try it and see.'

'I will!' said Dick. 'I'll do it! Ta very much, Orlando. I'm obliged to yer, mate.'

Orlando stood up to leave, and held out his hand to wish Dick good luck, but took it back before Dick touched it.

'Oh no,' he said. 'Better not. This hand can crush rocks. Cheerio, Dick, and the best of luck.'

Meanwhile, Benny was prowling up and down opposite the gasworks entrance, waiting for Mr Whittle to come out. His disguise made him impossible to recognize, of course, and he was almost invisible anyway because of the cat-like silence and swiftness of his movements. Only two nervous horses shied at his appearance, and only half-a-dozen ragamuffins with nothing better to do jeered at this strange painted figure with the flapping sleeves and the immense bowler hat; but he ignored them majestically. He was a tiger stalking its prey, and tigers take no notice of jackals.

Finally, at five past six, Mr Whittle appeared.

46

Benny pressed himself back into the shadows of the alley opposite the gasworks entrance, and watched with narrow eyes from under the brim of his hat as Mr Whittle stopped for a word with the watchman at the gate. The watchman touched his cap, Mr Whittle raised his cane in salute, and set off – towards Gas-Fitters' Hall.

Benny felt a thrill of excitement. Hitching up the trousers, which had started to unroll during the cat-like movements, and wrinkling his nose to keep the hat-brim up, he darted from the alley and crouched in concealment behind a dustbin, watching Mr Whittle like a hawk.

And so began a strange procession up Southwark Street, under the railway bridge, and left into Blackfriars Road. Mr Whittle sauntered along, looking the picture of innocence. You'd never think he was a desperate criminal. He raised his hat to Mrs Fanny Blodgett and Mrs Rosa Briggs, who were enjoying the evening sunshine outside Mrs Blodgett's Tea Rooms; he bought an evening paper from Charlie Rackett on the corner of Blackfriars Road; he even stopped for a genial word with P.C. Jellicoe.

But always behind him, darting from dustbin to horse-trough to cab-stand like a phantom of Vengeance, came the strangely garbed figure of Benny Kaminsky.

And with every step they got closer and closer to Gas-Fitters' Hall. When they were nearly there, Mr Whittle stopped and looked around, as if he were suspicious that someone might be following him. Benny was ready for that. He was only about ten feet away, and there was no dustbin to dodge behind, so he sauntered on past without making the slightest sign that he'd even noticed Mr Whittle.

Once he'd reached the bow window of the draper's shop a bit further along, he looked in it for the reflection of what was happening behind, and to his delight he saw Mr Whittle look around once more and step into the alley right next to Gas-Fitters' Hall. Benny could hardly contain himself, for that was the very alley in which they'd found the match.

Forgetting about the cat-like movements, he turned and pelted back to the alley at top speed, stopping just in time to peer round the corner first, in case Mr Whittle was waiting with a drawn revolver or a blackjack or a stiletto. But he wasn't. Instead, Benny saw his legs disappearing up a flight of iron stairs at the other end of the alley.

Almost yelping with excitement, Benny followed.

It seemed to be a kind of fire-escape. As far as Benny could see, it went right to the top, and he could hear the measured tread of Mr Whittle's boots ringing on the iron and moving up without a pause. He followed as quietly as he could, looking up all the time through the grille-like steps, and only twice fell over the unrolling trouser-legs. The second time, though, the bowler hat rolled off and nearly fell through the steps down to the alley below.

He grabbed it just in time and turned back upwards. Mr Whittle's footsteps weren't making any noise on the iron, and as Benny peered upwards through the gaps in the staircase he couldn't see the shape of Mr Whittle's body against the blue evening sky. Obviously he was lying in wait. Benny felt a tremor of apprehension. He tiptoed up the last flight of steps, which seemed to lead directly on to the roof. With enormous care he moved up until his eyes were level with the edge, and squinted from under the hat-brim with the hawk-like gaze of an Apache warrior.

The roof of Gas-Fitters' Hall was flat, with a little brick parapet around the edge. In the middle of it was a curious little hut, and outside the hut the great criminal was sitting on a wooden seat, stroking a pigeon which he held against his breast. A sound of soft cooing came from behind him.

'Hello, Benny,' said Mr Whittle.

'Er – I ain't Benny,' said Benny. 'He's – er – he's dead. I'm – er – someone else. Fred,' he said inspired. 'Fred Basket.'

Somehow the second name wasn't quite as good as the first, but there was nothing he could do about it now. Mr Whittle removed his hand from the pigeon and held it out solemnly. Benny cautiously shook it.

'How d'you do, Fred,' said Mr Whittle. 'Sorry to hear about Benny.'

'Yeah,' said Benny. 'They're all dead, all his family.'

'Really?'

'Yeah. The – er – the roof fell in and squashed 'em. They couldn't even tell which was which, they was so squashed.'

'Dear oh dear,' said Mr Whittle. 'I shall have to go somewhere else for my suits now. That's a great pity. Squashed, you say?'

'Yeah. There was blood and guts and bones all over the place. But they could tell which one was Benny, just.'

'Oh? How was that?'

'They found him holding up the roof. Or trying to. He was holding it up so the others could get out. Sorta like this . . .'

Benny demonstrated someone of gigantic strength struggling to resist an overpowering weight on his shoulders. He staggered – he groaned – he sank to his knees – he tried to rise again, but finally fell with a piteous cry. The bowler hat rolled off and lay unnoticed by the door of the hut.

'A heroic deed,' said Mr Whittle. 'How did they know it was him if everyone was squashed, though?'

'Cause just his face was left, sticking out the rubble. Here, Mr Whittle – '

Benny was becoming more and more intrigued by the pigeon sitting placidly in Mr Whittle's hands. He scrambled up, the squashed Kaminskys forgotten, and came to look at it.

'– is that a carrier pigeon?' he asked.

'It's a racing pigeon,' said Mr Whittle. 'I've been a little worried about this fellow. He's been off his food, but I think he's better now. Would you like to see the others?'

'Cor, yeah,' said Benny.

'Hold this one, then,' said Mr Whittle, and passed it to Benny, who held it gently against his chest as Mr Whittle opened the door of the hut. 'I've always kept pigeons,' Mr Whittle went on. 'I couldn't keep 'em at home, because they used to make my wife sneeze. When she died a few years back I suppose I could've moved the loft over to my house, but this arrangement seems to work pretty well. I pay a bit of rent to the Gas-Fitters' Company and everyone's happy. Here we are, then . . .'

The pigeon-loft was dark and warm and full of bird-like smells and noises. There was a row of neat little cages on each side, and about a dozen pigeons sat plumply on their perches.

'You want to help me feed 'em, Ben – er, Fred?' said Mr Whittle.

'Yeah!'

He took the pigeon from Benny and put it in its cage before giving Benny a little tin cup to scoop bird-seed out of a sack.

'About half a cupful each,' said Mr Whittle.

'Here, Mr Whittle,' said Benny, 'I bet you could train 'em to carry messages. They'd be a whole sight quicker'n the Post Office. Quicker'n a telegram, even.'

'I dare say,' said Mr Whittle.

'And *much* quicker'n a cab. You could have 'em flying all over London. They could deliver messages so quick you could make a fortune, probly. You could charge a penny a go. Or you could train really fast ones for threepence. Or you could train 'em to go and recruit other ones from Trafalgar Square! Or train a dozen of 'em to fly together and carry parcels . . . And every shop and company and factory could have a pigeon-loft on the roof and they'd have to pay rent for 'em like a telephone. Then you could start training some extra long-distance pigeons to fly to Paris and the Continent. And – and seagulls to fly to America. Or albatrosses, probly. You could have an albatross post office for across the sea and . . . Or even fish,' he said, completely carried away. 'You could train haddocks and that to swim with little waterproof bags. In a war that'd be dead useful, cause a haddock could go into an enemy harbour

51

and take messages from a spy. You could train 'em to come to a special underwater whistle . . . Probly get a medal for it from the Queen,' he said. 'Distinguished Haddock Cross.'

'You probably would,' said Mr Whittle. 'Look, I'm going to close up now, because it's time I went home. It's been a pleasure talking to you, Fred. I'm only sorry about the Kaminsky family. What a tragedy!'

'Yes,' said Benny distantly. He was beginning to regret the falling-house story. 'Course, it might not have been them after all,' he added. 'They were squashed so flat, it was hard to tell. It might've been a different family, and someone who just *looked* like Benny's face sticking out.'

'Yes, it might,' said Mr Whittle. 'And there's a lot of people look like Benny, after all. You look a bit like him yourself. You be careful down those stairs now.'

He closed the door of the pigeon-loft, which had an ordinary latch and no lock, and the two of them went down the iron staircase to the alley. Mr Whittle turned to Benny, shook hands, and wished him good evening before strolling off. Benny watched him thoughtfully.

He might have been downcast, because Mr Whittle was plainly not the thief after all, so they had to start again. On the other hand, he liked Mr Whittle, and he was glad to find him innocent. Even the fact that he'd been anxious about something was clear now – he'd been worried about his pigeon; and if *he* wasn't the thief, then someone else undoubtedly was. And that was worth knowing.

52

He was about to go back to the hideout and get out of his disguise, which was getting hotter and more uncomfortable by the minute, when he suddenly realized he hadn't got the bowler hat. Of course! It had come off when he was acting getting squashed, and rolled behind the door of the pigeon-loft.

He scratched his floury head. His sister Leah's young man Joe had taken a lot of persuading to lend his hat, and Benny didn't fancy the trouble he'd be in if the hat wasn't returned in good time, and in good shape too, come to that. He'd have to go back up and get it.

He climbed the staircase again. Not wanting to waste the chance, he became an albatross-trainer climbing a wild cliff-face to the albatross-loft in order to send his fastest albatross on a desperate mission across the Atlantic. He struggled against the wild wind and the lashing rain, clawing his way to the rocky summit of the cliffs and crawling on his stomach across the storm-beaten grass in order to avoid being swept off. He reached the albatross-loft and hauled himself up, gasping with effort, and lifted the latch and fell full-length inside, panting.

The albatrosses shifted on their perches and cooed anxiously.

Benny lay there for a minute to recover from the broken leg he'd sustained in a fall from half-way up the cliff, and then sat up, found the bowler hat absent-mindedly, and put it on. Time to feed the albatrosses, he thought. He gave each of them a haddock, and then rummaged behind the sack of bird-seed for the special waterproof message-pouch he was going to fix to the strongest albatross.

As his hands felt in the darkness he suddenly stopped and stood up.

Everything had gone silent and still. The albatrosses were forgotten. Benny's eyes, wide open, stared down past the sack of bird-seed as if they couldn't believe what was there.

Then he bent down again and carefully moved the sack away, and it was true, he hadn't dreamed it: behind the bird-seed was another sack, the top hanging open, and inside it was the faint gleam of silver. Great cups and bowls and plates, and in the middle a solid silver gas-fitter's wrench on an ebony plinth surmounted with silver laurel leaves. It was the loot from the robbery, and Mr Whittle had been hiding it after all.

Four

The Potted Palm

Benny shut the door of the pigeon-loft behind him and crept to the iron staircase, looking down to make sure the alley was clear. Seeing no sign of Mr Whittle, he cautiously climbed down, tiptoed out of the alley and ran away for the hideout as fast as he could.

He dodged through the stable, avoiding the automatic kick from Jasper the bad-tempered horse, clambered up the ladder, and found the hideout empty, to his relief. He took off the suit and rubbed his face on the lining of the jacket to get rid of the moustache, and succeeded, mostly. The suit itself was a little used-looking, mainly from being crawled across the roof in. He could brush it later, if he found a brush. The main thing was to get rid of the flour in his hair. It was no good washing it out; he'd tried that before, and the stuff turned into a very effective glue. For weeks afterwards he'd gone about with hair that made a light knocking sound when you tapped it, like cardboard, and mighty uncomfortable it was too, not to mention noisy. So he spent some time now shaking his head and running his fingers through his hair and rubbing it on the suit's trouser-legs until it was more or less its normal dingy brown again.

Then he prised a 'Monstroso' giant peppermint humbug away from the paper bag it was sticking to, wedged it firmly into his cheek as an aid to thought, and flung himself on the heap of straw in the corner to work out what to do next.

He hadn't been there long when the trapdoor lifted, and Thunderbolt peered in at him, looking excited.

'Here!' he said. 'Dick's gonna do it! He's got a love secret from Orlando the strong man, and he's gonna ask Daisy tonight! We're gonna win the bet after all!'

He clambered up, followed by the twins. Benny frowned austerely.

'And Snakes-Eyes don't know about Orlando's love secret, so he's offering five to one against Dick now,' said Angela. 'It's worth borrowing a fortune for!'

'Imagine that,' said Thunderbolt, his spectacles glowing. 'Five shillings for a one-bob stake! Cor . . .'

'Mmm,' said Benny. He shifted the humbug from one cheek to the other, gazing into the middle distance.

'What's the matter?' said Angela.

'You ain't put some money on old Horspath?' said Zerlina suspiciously.

Benny gave her a cold look. Finally the others realized that he had something else on his mind, and remembered what he'd been doing.

'How'd you get on with following Mr Whittle?' said Thunderbolt.

Benny took out the humbug, balanced it carefully on one knee, and began to explain. He had never had a better audience; they sat wide-eyed and open-mouthed.

'You *sure*?' said Thunderbolt when he'd finished.

'You saw all of it? All that loot?' said Angela.

'It wasn't just tools for pigeon-breeding?' said Zerlina.

'You don't breed pigeons with gas-fitters' wrenches made of solid silver,' said Benny scornfully. 'Nor you don't need blooming great dishes half a yard across to feed 'em with, neither. I fed 'em meself with a little tin cup about *that* big. Mr Whittle let me do it.'

'But why would he let you do that if there was all that loot stashed behind it?' said Thunderbolt. 'It's funny him letting you in there at all.'

'That's what I think,' said Benny. 'But I tell you one thing, I got a plan coming. I can feel it. I just need to work out the details. But it's a good 'un. It's one of the best I ever had. In fact, it's a blooming cracker.'

Thunderbolt looked at the twins, who looked apprehensively back at him and then at each other. They knew the signs. Benny's eyes were remote, as if he were staring at something too far-off for the others to see, and his lips were moving faintly.

'Yeah,' he said after a minute or so, detaching the humbug from the dusty fibres of his trouser-leg before tossing it into the air and catching it in his mouth with a gulp. 'This is gonna be a stunner. It's gonna be a corker. It's gonna be a knock-down sockdologer!'

'But –' Thunderbolt began.

Benny held up his hand. 'I need to get it right first. Get all the details straight. You better leave me alone for now, else I'll get it wrong. I need silence and being alone. Go on, hook it. I'll find yer when I've got it all worked out.'

'You don't want to put summing on Dick at Snake-Eyes's five to one?' said Angela, half-way out of the trapdoor.

'No. I got nothing left anyway. Go on, I mean it, I want to think about it on my own.'

So the others left. Benny heard Zerlina enthusiastically explaining to Thunderbolt on the way down that if he placed his next trigonometry shilling with Snake-Eyes Melmott as well as the first one, he'd have a total profit of seven shillings when Dick finally triumphed. Her eager voice died away as the others went out through the stable, and then there was silence, broken only by the continual buzz of flies around old Jasper below, the swish of his irritable tail, and the high-pitched, almost electrical hum that Benny felt must be coming from his mighty brain at full stretch.

Daisy had been puzzled and a little hurt by the fact that she hadn't seen Dick since the unfortunate incident in the Music Hall. She understood what had happened; the poor boy had got his words mixed up. It wasn't his fault he wasn't a smooth-tongued genius. But she couldn't wait for ever, and meanwhile Mr Horspath was being so charming and attentive . . . He had brought her a box of chocolates the day before, and he'd spent three-quarters of an hour listening to Daisy's mother telling him about her rheumatism, and he did have nice wavy fair hair, and . . .

And he was coming round that very evening to

have a meat tea with the family. When he accepted Mrs Miller's invitation, there was a kind of a warm meaningfulness in the way he smiled at Daisy that made her heart give a sickly lurch, as if it didn't know whether to go up or down.

So all that afternoon, as she wrapped cakes and sold biscuits and buttered buns in the bakery where she worked, she kept thinking of Dick and sighing, and thinking of Mr Horspath and smiling, and then smiling about Dick and sighing over Mr Horspath, till the silly girl didn't know who she loved and who she didn't. All she knew was that she must be in love with someone, or she wouldn't feel so miserable.

Thunderbolt, meanwhile, was undergoing the most powerful temptation of his life. He was on his way to the Whittles' house for his next trigonometry lesson with another shilling in his pocket, and there outside the Rose and Crown stood Snake-Eyes Melmott himself, talking to a couple of jockey-looking men.

The great bookmaker was a stout prosperous rosy-cheeked man, with a tight check suit, a curly-brimmed bowler hat, and a great gold watch-chain across his middle. He had a air about him of cigars and gold sovereigns, of horses and whisky, of large dinners and boxing-rings.

Thunderbolt slowed down as he went past. Then he stopped. Then he went on more slowly. Then he turned round.

Snake-Eyes Melmott was looking at him benevolently.

'How do, young Thunderbolt,' he said, and his voice was as rich as a plum pudding.

'How do, Mr Melmott,' said Thunderbolt. 'I was just wondering . . .'

'Ah, yes? Anything I can help you with?'

'Er – Dick Smith – you know the business with Daisy, and . . .'

'Mm-hmm.'

'I heard you were offering five to one.'

Snake-Eyes Melmott put his tongue in his cheek, looked around roguishly, leant forward, as far as his stomach would let him, and lowered his voice confidentially to say: 'Seeing as you're a good customer, Thunderbolt, and seeing as I've heard from the stable that Mr Horspath's making a very good showing, I can offer you six to one, my boy. Six to one against young Dick.'

Six to one! Thunderbolt glowed. Even the twins hadn't managed to get six to one from the great Snake-Eyes Melmott. It was too tempting to refuse. After all, if he won, he'd be eight shillings to the good, and he could pay for his own trigonometry lessons instead of asking Pa, and he could buy some flowers for Miss Whittle, and . . .

Out came the shilling; out came Snake-Eyes Melmott's little black betting book.

'So you got one bob at two to one, and another bob at sixes. I can see you're a shrewd betting man, young Thunderbolt. I shall have to watch my step with you. Remember the terms of the bet: Dick has got to propose to Daisy, and be accepted, by midnight on the 14th. That's two nights away – the night of the Gas-Fitters' Ball.'

Thunderbolt nodded. Snake-Eyes Melmott shook his hand and put away his little black book, and Thunderbolt moved on to the Whittles' house, feeling guilty and excited both at the same time.

And now for the first time he began to take in what Benny had said about Mr Whittle and the pigeon-loft and the stolen silver. He was so excited by the idea of winning more money on Dick that he hadn't remembered that he was going to walk into the house of a desperate criminal.

And as he waited for Miss Honoria Whittle in the dining-room, he realized what it would mean if Mr Whittle was arrested. Unlike Benny, he didn't believe that Miss Whittle was involved at all. Diamond Lou, with a revolver in her stocking! Huh! But that made him feel even guiltier about the shilling bet. That was two shillings he owed her now. She might need those two shillings to live on, if her father was in prison. What would Thunderbolt do if he saw her begging in the street? He'd feel too ashamed for words.

'Hello, Sam,' she said in her friendly way as she came in and sat down with him.

He gulped, and they began their lesson. But he found it hard to concentrate, and kept saying the most unfortunate things.

'Miss Whittle,' he said, 'd'you think your father would let me look after his pigeons, if –'

He stopped suddenly.

'If what, Sam?'

If he goes to prison, was what Thunderbolt had been going to say.

'If . . . if he needs any help,' he finished lamely.

'You could always ask him,' said Miss Whittle. 'Now what about that tangent, Sam? Have another look at it.'

A little later he said, 'Would someone get a longer prison sentence for stealing antique silver than just ordinary silver, miss?'

'I really don't know,' she said. 'What an odd question. Come on: what's the sine of an angle again? You must try and get it right.'

And finally he said, thinking aloud: 'I suppose Mr Whittle could always escape to Sweden . . .'

'What *are* you talking about?'

'Oh. Sorry, miss. I was just thinking.'

'Escape, did you say? Escape from what?'

'From a gang,' Thunderbolt made up quickly. 'Of – er – thieves. Or murderers, even. Seeing as he's been to Sweden already, he can probably speak Swede, I expect.'

'Your mind's certainly wandering today, Sam. What makes you think Papa's been to Sweden?'

'Hasn't he? I thought he went and made a speech to the European Gas and Coke and Congress and Manufacturers Council?'

'Oh, that! I see what you mean. No, he was going to go, but Mr Horspath went instead. Papa thought it would be a good experience for him.'

'Mr *Horspath?*' Thunderbolt goggled.

'Why, yes. Mr Horspath is the Deputy Manager, after all. He was very grateful for the opportunity.'

'Did he bring back any matches for Mr Whittle?'

'Matches?'

'Swedish ones. For Mr Whittle's cigars and that.'

'But Papa doesn't smoke. Dear me, Sam, you are

62

in a curious state this afternoon. What's all this about matches?'

'Oh! Er – umm – I collect 'em. For my museum. Different kinds of matches.'

'And why are you so interested in Mr Horspath?'

''Cause – cause he's courting Daisy Miller.'

'Ah, I see . . . But what about Dick Smith? The poor man with the phobia? Hasn't he managed to propose yet?'

Thunderbolt tried to collect his wits, and told her about the incident in the Music Hall. She laughed gently.

'Poor man! And Daisy too. A bowl of bananas, you say? Oh dear! No, it's not very tactful, is it.'

He wondered whether to tell her about the secret of love, as revealed by Orlando, but it was time to go; and in any case he was bursting to get back to the hideout, find Benny and the others, and tell them this astonishing news about Mr Horspath.

As for Mr Horspath himself, that elegant and wavy-haired gentleman was knocking on the door of the Millers' house at that very moment, clasping a large bunch of roses and wearing his best light tweed suit, with a purple cravat fastened in the fashionable new style with a little silver ring.

The Millers wanted to make a good impression on Mr Horspath, because he just might want to propose to Daisy, you never knew. Mr Miller had been made to put his best suit on, which made him hot and fidgety, and told to be polite and not pour his tea into the saucer to cool it, which made him cross.

'Blooming fuss,' he grumbled. 'What's the matter

with young Dick then? Why d'you want to marry this popinjay?'

'He's not a popinjay, Pa, he's a Deputy Gasworks Manager. And as for Dick, the less said the better,' said Daisy, who couldn't think of anything else to say about him anyway.

When Mr Horspath knocked at the door Mrs Miller was just rushing to the dining-table with a dish of beetroot salad.

'Oh! There he is! Daisy, come here – you got a smudge on your cheek. Albert, cut that ham nice and thin. And don't you *dare* do that silly trick with the cucumber. I shall die. Quick, Daisy! Open the door!'

Mr Horspath came in and shook hands all round, and presented Mrs Miller with the roses, and then they all sat down at the table to eat the substantial meat tea Mrs Miller and Daisy had prepared. There was ham and tongue and tinned salmon, there was beetroot and tomatoes and lettuce and cucumber, there was thin bread and butter, and there was strawberries and cream to follow.

'What a splendid repast!' Mr Horspath said.

'The re-past is all right,' said Mr Miller, 'but what about the re-future, eh?'

'Oh! Ha ha!' said Mr Horspath, showing his appreciation of Mr Miller's wit. 'Jolly good!'

Mr Miller was pleased to have his little joke laughed at, and went on: 'Here, Mr Horspath. Would you say this was a warm evening?'

'Jolly warm, yes. Splendid weather.'

'Now when I was in the Army,' said Mr Miller, 'out in India, we had a little dodge that we used to get up to to keep ourselves cool. What you do is –'

64

Mrs Miller kicked him on one ankle, and Daisy kicked him on another, but he had his best boots on, and they were pinching his toes so tightly that the kicks came as a welcome relief. He ignored them and went on.

'What you do is, you cut a nice long piece of cucumber peel, like this' – he cut one for himself, and handed another to Mr Horspath – ' and you stick it on your forehead. Go on, try.'

He stuck his own on, and Mr Horspath did the same with his. They sat there looking at each other.

'Remarkable cooling properties, cucumber,' said Mr Miller.

'Jolly cool, yes,' said Mr Horspath, nodding. The cucumber peel slid down his nose. He had the uncomfortable feeling that Mr Miller was laughing at him, though the other man was looking inscrutably solemn.

After the meal Mrs Miller said, 'Daisy, dear, do take Mr Horspath into the parlour. Your Pa and me has got things to do in the kitchen.'

The way she looked at her husband made it clear that she was going to tell him off about the cucumber business, but Mr Horspath pretended not to notice that and stood up politely to open the door for Daisy.

'This way, Mr Horspath,' said Daisy, who could have whacked her father over the head with his wretched cucumber. Every time she brought someone nice home, he had to go and make them stick cucumber peel all over themselves and look silly. She could have cried.

But Mr Horspath was so nice he didn't seem to mind.

'I say, Daisy,' he said when they were sitting on the little sofa, 'I wish you'd call me Bertie.'

'Oh, thank you!' said Daisy, shyly tweaking a frond of the enormous potted palm that stood behind the sofa. This potted palm was Mr Miller's pride and joy. He claimed he had grown it from a coconut that a monkey in India had thrown at him, but no one really believed that. It was so big now that it almost filled the space between the sofa and the window, and darkened the room considerably.

Mr Horspath sat a little closer and slid his arm along the back of the sofa behind Daisy.

'Daisy,' he murmured, 'I'm so glad we're alone at last. I've wanted to be alone with you for weeks and weeks . . .'

And she felt little shivers going all the way up and down her spine, as if mice were dancing on her. She even heard little mouse-like rustlings from somewhere in the room. How embarrassing! She hoped Mr Horspath wouldn't notice.

All this time, the twins had been preparing the way for Dick to unleash the power of Orlando's love secret. Knowing nothing about Mr Horspath's visit to the Millers', they had arranged for Dick to crouch unseen behind the privet hedge in the Millers' little front garden, and then clamber through the front window like a lover in a play. Daisy often sat in the parlour of an evening, and he could make his declaration of love without being interrupted.

So very, very carefully and quietly Angela raised the window and held aside the thick palm-leaves that got in the way.

'Look,' she whispered, 'there's her hand already, on the back of the sofa. All you gotta do is grab it and cover it with burning kisses.'

Dick, trembling with resolution, stepped through with no more noise than a mouse. He could see the hand where Angela was pointing – a soft, delicate, pale hand. It could only be Daisy's. He was nearly there!

'Go *on*,' whispered Zerlina.

Dick nodded, took a deep breath, closed his eyes, and grabbed.

What happened next was never entirely clear to anyone.

First, the potted palm fell over with a mighty crash.

Then Daisy gave a yell of alarm.

Then Mr Horspath stood up in horror and gazed open-mouthed at his own right hand, which was being covered with burning kisses by a blushing Dick, whose eyes were screwed tight shut.

Before anyone could speak, Dick (who'd been counting) came to the twelfth burning kiss and pressed Mr Horspath's hand to his heart.

'I loves yer!' he bawled hoarsely. 'Will yer marry me?'

'WHAT?' shrieked Mr Horspath.

Dick opened his eyes.

His jaw fell.

He looked at Mr Horspath, at Daisy, at the potted palm, at his own hand, still clutching Mr Horspath's. He let go as if it was electrified.

'You snake in the grass!' he shouted, and punched Mr Horspath right on the nose.

Angela and Zerlina cheered loudly.

'Go it, Dick!' they cried. 'Whack him again!'

Mr Horspath clutched his nose with a shrill cry, and then events got out of control, as the twins told Benny and Thunderbolt later.

Unknown to anyone, P.C. Jellicoe had been passing by, and hearing the noise of a disturbance of the peace, he blew his whistle vigorously and lumbered to the scene.

Mr and Mrs Miller heard the noise too, even over their discussion of the cucumber business, and came hurrying in to see what was going on.

They found Mr Horspath trying to mop his nose and hide behind Daisy while Dick chased him furiously, waving his fists.

'Come on out and fight, you wavy-haired weasel!' Dick roared.

'No – no – help!' cried Mr Horspath. 'He's assaulting me! Help!'

'Stop it, Dick! Stop it!' cried Daisy.

'Help! Police!' shouted Mrs Miller. 'Murder!'

'Go on, Dick, clock him another one,' said Mr Miller, but then he saw the ruins of his potted palm, and struck his forehead in horror. 'My potted palm!' he shouted. 'I grew that meself from a coconut! Who's done that? Was that you, Horsface?'

'No!' sobbed Mr Horspath, dodging behind Daisy again. 'It was him!'

'Come here! Come out and take yer medicine!' bellowed Dick, bouncing up and down and waving his fists. 'Making up to Daisy like that! Blooming sauce! I'll teach yer to – '

But what Dick intended to teach Mr Horspath

they never heard, because P.C. Jellicoe, looking in at the window, blew such a blast on his whistle that they all fell still with their ears ringing.

'Woss going on?' P.C. Jellicoe demanded. 'Is this a private and domestic dispute, or do you require the assistance of the law?'

'Constable, arrest this man!' blubbered Mr Horspath. 'And as for your position at the Gasworks, Smiss, you can consider yourself dismithed!'

'Eh?' said Daisy.

'You can't do that!' said Dick. 'This ain't nothing to do with the blooming Gasworks – this is a matter of love and honour!'

'I can do what I like,' said Mr Horspath, mopping his nose, feeling a bit safer now that P.C. Jellicoe had clambered in through the window to protect him. 'And you heard what I said. You're sacked!'

With a roar, Dick sprang at him again. He managed to get in one good wallop. Mr Horspath went down with a shriek, and then P.C. Jellicoe got the handcuffs on Dick, who was struggling like an eel.

Outside the window, in the shadow of the privet hedge, the twins looked at each other. They didn't need to speak. Leaving the confusion of wailing and shouting and banging behind them, they softly and suddenly vanished away.

'So he's arrested,' said Angela.

'In *gaol*?' said Benny.

'Yeah!' said Zerlina. 'We watched old Jelly-Belly drag him away in handcuffs. Half the street was watching!'

'So . . .' Thunderbolt gulped. 'If he's in gaol . . .

He can't ask Daisy to ... And the Gas-Fitters' Ball's the day after tomorrow . . .'

'Did you put that other shilling on with Snake-Eyes?' said Angela.

He nodded speechlessly.

'Cor,' said Zerlina.

They looked at him with pity and wonder, as if he were a ruined man already. Thunderbolt felt the shadow of the workhouse looming over him – and worse. He was thinking of the melodrama he and Pa had been to see the week before called 'The Primrose Path, or If Only He Had Known', in which a fine young man descended step by easy step along the road to ruin. Drink; low companions; loose women, whatever they were; and – Thunderbolt gulped – it had all started with gambling. The young man in the play had begun by betting the rent money on a horse-race and ended up on the gallows, and the last scene of all showed his poor mother weeping in the snow outside the prison walls as the bell tolled eight o'clock, the execution hour.

Thunderbolt opened his mouth once or twice, but couldn't speak. Suddenly that felt like his future, too.

'Right,' said Benny. 'We gotta do summing about this. You two gotta get Dick out of gaol, cause you got him in. Oh yes you blooming did,' he went on hotly as the twins started to argue. 'Never mind blooming Snake-Eyes Melmott and five to one and winning fortunes and so on. Dick's in gaol and he didn't oughter be and you gotta get him out. I don't care what you do – you make sure he's there at the Gas-Fitters' Ball. Meanwhile, me and Thunderbolt's got summing even more difficult and dangerous to do. We might end up in gaol ourselves for it, but it's gotta be done. It wouldn't be right otherwise. So there,' he finished, glaring around pugnaciously. 'Anyone arguing? Good. Now let's get on with it!'

Five

The Ladder

The twins weren't allowed to know what Benny and Thunderbolt were doing, in case they were caught and tortured. If they didn't know, they couldn't confess.

'Like Garibaldi and the Redshirts,' said Angela, 'fighting the Austrians.'

There was an engraved portrait of the great Italian hero above the sideboard in their parlour. They'd never been entirely clear about what he'd done, but they were sure it was very gallant and dangerous.

As their task was now. They walked home slowly, talking under their breath, leaning together slightly in the curious way they did when they were plotting something. More than one person who saw them crossed their fingers superstitiously, having seen them in action before.

At supper they hardly noticed what they were eating. Their mother had to bang the table and reach meaningfully for the breadknife before they came out of their mutual trance.

'What's up, gals?' said their father, a cheerful soul.

'Nothing,' said Angela.

'They're in trouble,' said their brother Alf. 'I can tell.'

'No we ain't,' said Zerlina.

'Well, if they're not yet, they're gonna be,' said their other brother Giuseppe, or Joe for short. Like their father, he worked in the dried-fruit trade.

'They get in a trouble, I cut a their troats,' said their mother, feeling the edge of the breadknife. Most of the Peretti men who'd been born in London used to go back to Naples to find a wife, which was why they spoke better English than Italian, and their wives spoke better Italian than English.

'I should cut 'em anyway,' suggested Giuseppe. 'Save time. Here, Alf, fancy a stroll down the Walk later on? We might have a drink with Orlando.'

The twins felt a little shiver of excitement, and, because they were twins, each of them knew that the other had felt it at the same moment. The same cat-like smile appeared on their faces, and they turned their attention to the lasagne.

Much later, when darkness had fallen over Lambeth, when the hissing naphtha-lamps of the market stalls had all been put away, when only the grimy moon-light glimmered on the rough bricks and the dirty cobbles, two small figures trudged along beside the great grim wall of the prison.

Their heads were bowed; each of them held a big white handkerchief to her face; occasionally a sniff or even a broken sob would make its way out.

Just as they reached the little iron-studded oak door that was set into a big and even more iron-studded oak gate, a key turned, and the door creaked open. It was midnight: the hour when the prison warders changed shifts.

The little figures looked up tragically at the first man who came out. He was a big, ponderous man with a grey moustache, and when he saw the two girls gazing up at him imploringly, with the moon-

74

light glittering on the tears on their cheeks, he couldn't help stopping.

'What's the matter?' he said.

'It's our brother,' said Angela.

'He in here, is he?'

Angela gave a little sob and hid her face in the handkerchief. The warder shifted his feet uncomfortably, for he too had been to see 'The Primrose Path', and had found it as moving as Thunderbolt did.

'He's . . . He's not a bad man,' said Zerlina piteously, 'but he's passionate and impetuous.'

'And now we're all alone,' said Angela.

'We just want to know where he is,' said Zerlina, 'so we can wave to him and . . . and . . .'

'And pray for him,' Angela put in quickly.

'That's it, yeah,' said Zerlina. 'If only we knew which cell he was in we could feel a bit easier in our minds.'

'Cause we could come and just look up and . . . and think about him,' said Angela brokenly.

The warder felt a lump in his throat. He coughed hard.

'What's his name?' he said as sternly as he could manage.

'Dick Smith,' said Zerlina. 'He's not a *bad* man. He *means* good.'

'Ah, yes, Smith,' said the warder. 'Number 1045. He's in the East Wing. That's round here. You follow me, gals, and I'll show yer.'

He led them round the corner of the great grim wall and pointed to a tiny window high up under the edge of the roof.

'That's his cell, the third on the left,' he said. 'You could wave to him from here.'

'Oh, thank you, sir, thank you!' said Angela.

'You're a kind and noble man!' said Zerlina.

The warder brushed a manly tear from his eye. What a pair of angels!

'Well, I must say,' he said, 'he's a lucky feller to have such devoted sisters. I shouldn't wonder but what your love and devotion wouldn't make all the difference to a young lad like him. A good example like that might set him on the road to reform.' He began to walk off, and turned back to say, 'Who knows? With your help, he might not be in here for long!'

Oddly enough, that was exactly what the twins had in mind.

Their next stop was Charlie Ladysmith's builder's yard, next to the Candle Manufactory. It was locked, of course, in the middle of the night, but there was a loose panel in the wooden fence, and it only took a moment for the girls to slip through.

'You know what?' whispered Angela. 'They oughter make things like this for cats to come in through doors with.'

'No one'd buy 'em,' said Zerlina. 'It's a silly idea.'

'Yeah, perhaps it is. Now where's he keep them ladders?'

Charlie Ladysmith wasn't a very tidy builder, or he'd have repaired his fence by this time, but it didn't take long to find his ladders. They were leaning against the wall of the main shed, long ones, short ones, stepladders and platform ladders.

'Cor,' whispered Angela. 'They're blooming

long, all of 'em. Even the short ones is long.'

'How we gonna get one of them out?' said Zerlina.

It turned out to be easier than they'd thought. They only knocked over a pile of bricks, smashed a window, tipped a rain-water barrel over on to a heap of sand, jabbed a hole in the wall of the shed, and broke two more panels on the fence; and after twenty minutes' struggling, they had the longest ladder they could manage outside in the street.

'He better preciate this,' said Zerlina, panting. 'He better be grateful.'

Angela's eyes glittered with the thought of what they'd do to Dick if he didn't and wasn't. But they didn't have time to think about that; they had another call to make that night.

Being in the theatrical profession, The Mighty Orlando was used to staying in boarding-houses. There were good ones and bad ones. When he was working in London, he always stayed at Mrs Drummond's in Tower Street, where the landlady looked after him well, providing two loaves, three dozen eggs and five pounds of bacon for breakfast every day, as well as an extra strong bed to sleep in and a nice quiet room overlooking the back yard.

It was half-past one in the morning when the twins clambered over the wall into that very back yard, and looked up at the house, wondering which window was Orlando's.

It wasn't hard to tell, actually. Since it was a warm night, all the windows were open, and out of one of them came a snoring so thunderous that the twins were lost in admiration.

77

'Like an elephant!' said Angela.

'Or a railway engine. It's colossal!'

'How we gonna wake him up? Whatever noise we make, he won't hear it cause of the noise he's making hisself!'

In the end they threw stones through the window. Orlando was used to cannon-balls landing on his head, of course, so he hardly noticed a few pebbles; but finally, by luck, one of them landed in his open mouth. He swallowed it like a fly and woke up.

The twins heard the snoring stop with a sort of gulping noise. A moment or two later, Orlando appeared at the window, with a big white night-cap keeping the draughts off his shiny head.

'Who's that?' he said, peering down. 'Oh, it's you, gals. What can I do for yer?'

'Rescue someone from prison,' said Angela.

'It's easy,' said Zerlina. 'It'll only take ten minutes, honest.'

'Only if he's been unjustly accused,' said Orlando sternly. 'I takes a dim view of any hanky-panky with the law.'

'It's Dick,' said Angela. 'You remember that love secret you told him?'

'Yeah. How'd he get on?'

'He kissed the wrong hand and proposed to Mr Horspath by mistake,' said Zerlina, 'and they put him in gaol.'

Orlando was appalled.

'That's a monstrous piece of injustice!' he said, struggling into his clothes. 'I never heard the like! And it's my fault, and all. I oughter told him the first part of the love secret.'

'What's that?'

'Make sure you got hold of the proper hand. It's an easy mistake to make, especially when you're flustered. I spect Dick was a bit flustered. That's probly how it happened.'

They were all speaking in whispers, not wanting to wake the other lodgers. Orlando tiptoed downstairs and out of the kitchen door, and a few moments later they were on their way to prison. The twins told him more about the potted palm and Dick's unfortunate accident.

Orlando shook his head in dismay.

'I knew a trapeze artist once as made a similar mistake,' he said. 'Course, grabbing hold of the wrong hand in that profession is the last thing you want to do. Matter of fact, I think it was the last thing he *did* do. Where's this prison, then?'

They reached the prison, and the twins retrieved the ladder from the alley nearby where they'd left it.

'It's that window at the end,' whispered Angela.

'All right,' said Orlando. 'Now you two better keep watch in case a copper comes along. I shouldn't wonder but what he might think it was a bit suspicious.'

And he propped the ladder against the wall and began to climb up.

Dick was lying on his bunk dreaming of Daisy and Mr Horspath. She was telling him to put slices of cucumber on his black eye, and he was saying, 'Daisy, your face is like the moon rising over the Gasworks! Marry me at once!'

Dick growled in his sleep. Couldn't he even have a dream without that silky-handed stoat turning up in it?

So he was pleased to hear a knocking at the bars of his cell, and to wake up and see a broad-shouldered figure outlined against the dark sky.

'Psst!' came a mighty whisper. 'Dick!'

'Who's that? That's not Orlando, is it? What you doing here?'

'I come to rescue yer,' said Orlando. 'You better stand back. I can't answer for the strength of these walls.'

And he took hold of the bars and pulled them apart as if they were made of pastry. There was a great wrenching noise, and bricks and bits of stone fell down.

'Cor,' breathed Dick. 'Blimey!'

'Out yer come, then,' said Orlando.

'Can I come too?' said a shaky voice from the lower bunk, and a furtive-looking little man peered out, blinking and scratching his head.

'Who's that?' said Orlando, peering in.

'That's Sid the Swede,' said Dick. 'We turned out to be sharing a cell.'

'Oh, go on,' said Sid the Swede. 'Be a sport.'

He sat up and clasped his hands pleadingly.

'What you in here for?' said Orlando sternly. 'I ain't letting dangerous criminals out, only honest men what's been wrongly convicted.'

'I stole a couple of pillow-cases off a washing-line,' said Sid the Swede.

'What for?'

But before Sid the Swede could answer that, a

bell began to ring loudly, and pounding feet were heard running along the corridors towards the cell.

'That's the alarm!' said Dick. 'They must've heard you tearing the bars out, Orlando!'

'No time to waste, then,' said Orlando. 'You come down the ladder first, Dick, and then I'll let this gentleman out, being as he seems harmless enough. But mind,' he said, wagging a massive finger at Sid the Swede, 'any further law-breaking, and I shall be sorely disappointed in you. I couldn't answer for my temper in that case.'

'Yes! Yes! Anything!' squeaked Sid the Swede. 'I promise!'

So Orlando moved down the ladder, and Dick clambered out after him, and finally, hopping and squirming and yelping with fear, Sid the Swede came too.

'Quick! Quick!' the twins were calling, for a policeman's whistle was blowing from the very next street.

Orlando and the two escaped convicts got to the bottom and scampered away after the two girls, not pausing for breath till they were safely back near the New Cut Gang's hideout over the stable. There they stopped, panting and triumphant.

'We never took Charlie Ladysmith's ladder back,' said Angela.

'Never mind,' said Zerlina, 'he'll be famous. Folks'll buy him drinks for days on account of having his ladder nicked for the great break-out.'

'But what am I going to do, gals?' said Dick. 'I mean, I'm glad to be out, and all, but I can't live the life of a fugitive. I'm a law-abiding bloke.'

'Yeah, so am I,' said Sid the Swede eagerly. 'I

never been in trouble in me life. I shall have to clear me name, else I shan't be able to hold me head up.'

'And how are you gonna do that?' said Orlando.

'I shall just have to tell the truth about the pillow-case business,' said Sid the Swede. 'No matter what the cost to my dignity. I value my reputation for truth and honesty. Well, goodnight all. And thank you, Mr – Whatever. You're a gentleman.'

He held out his hand to Orlando, who shook his head.

'No, no,' he said, 'better not. Find a rock and I'll show yer why.'

'Another time, perhaps, eh?' said Sid the Swede, and scuttled away.

'You better stay in the hideout tonight, Dick,' said Angela. We'll bring you some breakfast in the morning.'

'You only got to keep out the way till tomorrow night, anyway,' said Zerlina.

'Why?'

''Cause it's the Gas-Fitters' Ball tomorrow, and you're going,' said Angela. 'Everyone's gotta be there. And you can go in costume if you like, with a mask.'

Dick's mouth opened and closed, but no words came out of it.

'Anyway,' said Zerlina, 'we got another plan, ain't we, Ange?'

'Oh, yeah,' said Angela. 'We thought of it when you was up the ladder arguing. It's the best one yet. You'll be amazed, I promise.'

'Now get in quick, and stay clear of Jasper. He's bad-tempered at both ends.'

'All right,' said Dick meekly. 'I dunno what it is about you gals, I just can't argue with yer. Can you, Orlando?'

'I never could argue with a lady,' said the strong man, watching the girls run off into the dark as quick as sparks up a chimney. 'Well, good night, Dick. I'll see you at the Ball.'

Six

The Lambeth Bandit

All over Lambeth, people were getting ready for the Gas-Fitters' Ball.

The musicians of the Prince of Wales's Own Light Bombardiers, who were going to play for the dancing, were polishing their trombones and tightening their drums; the caterers were making ice-creams and soups and custards and pies and sandwiches of every sort; dressmakers were tightening straps and loosening waistbands and hemming edges and sewing on lace.

And the detectives from Scotland Yard, under the direction of Inspector Gorman, were making no progress at all with the case of the Gas-Fitters' Hall silver.

'All the usual villains seem to be on holiday, Inspector,' said the Sergeant.

'Well, try the unusual ones,' said the Inspector crossly. 'Try everyone.'

'What about Sid the Swede and this prison breakout last night?'

'Yes,' said the Inspector, scratching his chin. 'Sid couldn't have nicked the silver, but it's a curious business. The other bloke who got out was some young gas-fitter convicted of assault and battery . . .' Then he realized what he'd said. 'A gas-fitter!'

The two policemen looked at each other, wide-eyed.

'You don't think *he* could have been involved in the burglary?' said the Sergeant.

'Well, it's highly suspicious, to say the least. When he turns up, we better pull him in for questioning.'

'D'you think he will turn up, Inspector?'

'Of course! Scotland Yard always gets its man. There's dozens of trained sleuths looking for him right now, not to mention bloodhounds. He won't be free for long. And when he's put away next time, it'll be for a good long stretch.'

At that very moment, Dick was sitting in the gang's hideout chewing a stale currant bun and washing it down with a bottle of cold tea, and trying not to think about policemen. The twins had brought the food to him early that morning, and they were now basking in Benny's praise.

'You done all right,' he said, 'and no error. That must've took some doing, organizing a jail-break. Course me and Thunderbolt could've done it ourselves, only we had summing even harder to do.'

'What was that then?' said Angela.

'I better not tell you yet,' said Benny, 'on account of being caught and tortured. You'll find out tonight. But it was desperate and dangerous. And daring. I don't suppose anyone's been as daring as what Thunderbolt and me was last night.'

'Yes, they have,' said Zerlina. 'Me and Ange was. We fooled a prison warder into revealing where Dick was locked up –'

'And we borrowed a ladder from a builder's yard under the nose of a powerful bulldog with jaws *that* big –' said Angela.

'What we had to tame and master with special Italian dog-commands as made it roll over and keep quiet –'

'And we smuggled Orlando out his boarding-house wrapped in a roll of carpet –'

'And we fought off three policemen what tried to capture the ladder Dick was coming down –'

'Did you really?' said Thunderbolt, deeply impressed. 'Cor.'

'Yeah, all right, all right,' said Benny impatiently. 'We *all* been daring and desperate.'

'Yeah,' said Dick, swallowing the last of the currant bun. 'I reckon you have, kids. But I'm wondering what I ought do next, cause I'm on the run now, ain't I? I'm a wanted man. There's probly a price on me head.'

'Better be a big 'un,' said Angela, 'the trouble we went through. They better not offer just half a crown.'

'In Sicily,' said Zerlina, 'when someone breaks out of jail, they go up in the hills and join the bandits and live in a cave.'

'Not many hills in Lambeth,' said Dick. 'Nor caves neither. I dunno if Daisy'd want to live in a cave, somehow.'

'She would if you asked her,' said Angela.

'Course she would,' said Zerlina. 'Cause she'd listen to you with a lot more respect if you was a bandit. She'd have to. Else you'd shoot her.'

'Or cut her froat,' said Angela.

'Well – ' began Dick.

'And you'd be able to ask her, too! You know the reason you couldn't ask her before?' said Zerlina.

'Yeah. I was too blooming shy,' said Dick.

'No! The *real* reason was, you was a gas-fitter. If you was a bandit, you wouldn't be nervous of nothing. You'd be bold and daring.'

'Would I?'

'Course you would,' said Angela.

And it was true, too. Dick felt himself become braver, more desperate, more daring, just by thinking about it. Dick Smith, a Wanted Man! Dangerous Dick Smith, The Lambeth Bandit!

'Yeah,' he said. 'I reckon you're right. I could do anything now! If Daisy was here I'd – I'd propose to her on the spot. No error!'

'Well, wait till tonight,' said Benny, 'cause you can do it at the Ball. You gotta be in disguise, of course. With a mask. And what *we* gotta do,' he said to the rest of the gang, 'is we gotta be there and all. We can work in the kitchens or summing. Cause everything's gonna happen tonight. The Gas-Fitters' Hall burglar's gonna be revealed!'

'And Dick's going to win his bet!' said Thunderbolt.

'Eh? What bet?' said Dick.

There was an awkward silence. Everyone looked at Thunderbolt, who suddenly realized what he'd said, and corrected himself quickly.

'I mean, propose to Daisy,' he said. 'I didn't mean bet at all. I was thinking of something quite different. I didn't mean Dick had made a bet on it. I mean, I didn't mean *anyone* had made a bet on it. I mean, proposed to Daisy. I mean –'

'Oh, stow it,' said Benny, 'we got no time for riddles. We gotta go and see the caterer and get ourselves jobs. You keep out of sight, Dick, remember, you're on the run. You can't slip out and have half a pint down the Feathers. If you get thirsty you'll have to wait till we bring you another bottle of tea or summing. And yer costume for later. I tell yer, mates, this is the best plan I ever had! This is a stunner!'

'And we got a plan and all,' said Zerlina smugly. 'Ain't we, Ange?'

But they refused to say what it was, in case of torture.

Daisy didn't know whether to feel more sorry for Dick, or for Mr Horspath with his spectacular black eye, or herself. In the end she felt sorry for all three of them in turn.

Another thing she didn't know was whether or not to go to the Ball. Mr Horspath had asked her, but she thought that Dick *would* have asked her if he'd got round to it, and she'd rather go with him; on the other hand, Dick was in gaol and Mr Horspath wasn't, and Mr Horspath had brought her a huge bunch of lilies only that morning and asked her again to go with him; and altogether the poor girl was scarcely in her right mind.

'I just dunno what to do, Ma!' she said after work.

'There, there, dear,' said Mrs Miller. 'If I was you I'd go with that nice Mr Horspath. He's a real gentleman.'

'I wouldn't if *I* was her,' said Mr Miller darkly. 'I don't think she'd be safe in his hands. A man what can treat a potted palm in that shocking and cold-blooded way is capable of any villainy.'

So Daisy dithered, and she might have gone on

dithering for ever if Angela hadn't called, late in the afternoon, with a message for her ears only.

'I can't stop long,' said Angela breathlessly when they were in the parlour, 'but I came to say you gotta go to the Ball, cause Dick's going to be there in disguise. He escaped from prison specially. Not even prison walls could keep him away from you. Not even crocodiles or machine-guns either, probly. And anyway you gotta be there for – for a special other reason. I gotta go now, but you *better* be there, or else.'

'Yes! Right! I will!' said Daisy. She was thrilled.

Angela scampered off, and Daisy shot upstairs to put on her ball dress.

And in every household in Lambeth, almost, people were putting on their finery. Some were going in fancy dress, and some weren't, because you could choose which you liked. Most of the younger people were going in costume, but the more respectable ones went in ordinary evening dress.

Mr Horspath, as a Deputy Gasworks Manager, thought he'd better be respectable, so he put on a white tie and black tail-coat, and anointed his hair with Bandoline to keep it in place and maintain the waviness people found so attractive. He had wondered what to do about his black eye until he found an advertisement in the Gentlemen's Gazette, and hurried along at once to Mr George Paul, of Oxford Street, an Artist in Black Eye. Mr Paul covered the wounded organ with theatrical make-up, and charged Mr Horspath half-a-crown for it; and now, as he peered into the mirror, it looked almost normal again. Daisy would be tremendously impressed, he thought, and he practised a specially charming smile two or three times till he got it right.

The Kaminskys were all going, too. Mr Kaminsky and Cousin Morris had spent hours arguing about whether or not the latest style in evening wear, the 'dress lounge', was suitable for such a high-toned affair as the Gas-Fitters' Ball.

'A tailor's got to innovate, Louis!' said Cousin Morris. 'He's got to be at the forefront of fashion!'

'No, no, no,' said Mr Kaminsky. 'A tailor's got to reflect the quiet good taste of traditional opinion. It's no good flaunting all your latest American fashions, not in Lambeth, anyway. You wear that dress lounge if you want to; I'm sticking to formal evening wear. Look at the cut of this waistcoat, now! Look at the shine on that lapel, eh! A thing of beauty is a joy forever, Morris.'

In the Dobney household, Thunderbolt's Pa was ironing his best trousers. Thunderbolt had wanted his father to go as a pirate, but Pa said he'd only worn this suit three times and hardly got his money's worth out of it; so he fetched it out of the wardrobe and set the iron on the stove and got to work. A pungent smell of mothballs was filling the little kitchen. Or *was* it mothballs?

Mr Dobney sniffed.

'Can you smell burning, Sam?' he said.

'Cor, yeah!' said Thunderbolt in alarm. 'You got the iron too hot, Pa! Take it off quick!'

Mr Dobney snatched the iron off his trousers just in time, and scratched his head.

'I dunno what it is, I can't seem to get it right. Your Ma never used to have any trouble with it.'

'What Mrs Malone does,' said Thunderbolt, 'she puts a wet cloth on it and irons through that. It goes all steamy.'

'Ah,' said Mr Dobney. 'I knew there was a secret to it.'

He put the iron back on the range to keep hot and dipped his handkerchief in the dishwater. This time the iron hissed and steamed properly, and beautiful sharp creases appeared down the trouser-legs.

'Smashing,' said Mr Dobney admiringly. 'You could slice a cucumber with them creases.'

The Peretti brothers, meanwhile, were criticizing each other's costumes. Alf was going as a gondolier, but he had so many rings in his ears and fake jewellery all over him that Giuseppe said he looked more like a chandelier.

'No, no, you got to be a bit showy,' said Alf. 'Make the best of yerself. The young ladies like a bit of show. I can't see 'em being impressed by them great caterpillars on your legs.'

Guiseppe was going as a cowboy, with a ten-gallon hat he could only just get through the door and huge furry chaps over his trousers.

'No, this is the tough and manly look,' he said. 'If it's good enough for Buffalo Bill, it's good enough for me.'

Alf twiddled his moustache and smirked.

And finally, in the Whittle household, Miss Honoria was pinning a gardenia to her ball gown. The flower had arrived by special messenger, with a card that said 'From an unknown admirer', and she hoped that if she wore it to the Ball, she might find out who had sent it.

'Very pretty, my dear,' said Mr Whittle. 'It's a shame you've only got your old father to go to the Ball with.'

'Not at all, Papa, you look very handsome,' said Miss Whittle, kissing his cheek and adjusting his bow tie.

So everyone was ready for the Ball.

'What's this plan of yours, then?' said Benny to the twins, as they hurried towards the kitchen entrance of Gas-Fitters' Hall.

'Ah ha,' said Angela. 'It's the best one yet.'

'You remember the Archbishop of Canterbury stunt?' said Zerlina.

'What, when you got the Archbishop to come and judge the cat show? That was a laugh, that was. Is he coming to the Ball, then?'

'No,' said Angela.

'Well, who is?' said Thunderbolt, bewildered.

'Ah ha,' said Zerlina. 'You wait and see.'

'You never got anyone!' said Benny.

'Betcher,' said the twins together.

The boys looked at each other. Never bet against the twins, was Benny's rule through life.

'H'mm,' was all he could find to say.

'Yes,' said Angela contentedly as they moved on. 'I bet you never had such a surprise as what we arranged tonight.'

'Oh yeah? Well, I bet our surprise is better'n yours,' retorted Benny, forgetting his lifelong rule at once.

However, there was no time to think of surprises once the work began. Benny and Thunderbolt were going to be pageboys, and the twins were going to help in the cloakroom, so they'd all be able to keep an eye on what was going on.

Gas-Fitters' Hall had been decorated in grand style. The ballroom was festooned with flowers and ribbons; dainty little tables and chairs were set along the sides, and a table as long as a cricket pitch was covered in a snowy white cloth on which stood piles of gleaming plates, lines of sparkling glasses, and boxes of silver cutlery for the buffet supper later on. On the bandstand, the musicians of the Prince of Wales's Own Light Bombardiers were taking their places, under the direction of their conductor, Lieutenant-Colonel Fidler. The dancing floor had been polished till it shone like silk.

In the kitchen, squads of cooks and under-cooks were putting the final touches to the salmon in aspic, the veal-and-ham pies, the Madeira trifles. The wine waiters were polishing their corkscrews, the ordinary waiters were smoothing down the white napkins over their left forearms, and the head waiter was calculating how much he was likely to get in tips. Everything was ready.

The first guests began to arrive soon after eight o'clock. The twins were interested to see how many of them had come in evening dress, and how many in costume. Four Demon Kings arrived in the first ten minutes, and four Gypsy Maidens, and they all stood round awkwardly trying not to look at each other until more people arrived.

'There's Alf and Giuseppe, look!' said Angela, as their big brothers came swaggering in. 'And who's that in the Arab Chieftain get-up?'

A figure dressed in white robes from head to foot

was shuffling into the ballroom. The robes were a bit too big for him, or he was a bit too small for them, and he tripped and fell full length.

'He's going to make a big impression,' said Zerlina. 'On the floor, anyway.'

'Here, look! Mr Horspath!'

Mr Horspath came in smiling widely, ran a careless hand over his hair to check that the waves were all still in place, and handed his top hat and gloves to Zerlina.

'Here you are, my girl,' he said. 'Look after them well, and there might be a sixpence for you.'

And he went into the ballroom, smiling at everyone in sight.

'I thought he was going with Daisy?' said Angela.

'Here's Daisy now, with her Pa and Ma,' said Zerlina.

When they'd checked in their hats, Mr Miller leaned over confidentially and asked Angela, 'D'you happen to know if they're serving salad with the refreshments?'

'Yeah,' she said. 'Full of cucumbers.'

'Good, good,' he said happily, and strolled into the ballroom.

While Mrs Miller went to attend to her hair, Zerlina told Daisy about Dick.

'He's coming as a bandit,' she said, 'with a black mask on. He's not here yet. I'll tell you as soon as he arrives.'

Daisy was looking very pretty indeed. In fact she was the prettiest young lady there by a long way, and as soon as he saw her, Mr Horspath immediately left the other young lady he'd been talking to and made straight for Daisy as if he was on rails.

'Miss Miller! Daisy!' he said. 'I'm so glad you could come! Do let me have the first dance.'

'Well,' she said, 'I dunno really.'

'But the musicians are striking up! The night is young! And how beautiful you look in your – Yes? What is it?'

There was a small, untidy pageboy plucking at his sleeve.

'Sandwich, guvnor?' said the pageboy, holding up a plate of them and shoving up some remarkably dirty spectacles.

'Oh, yes, yes, all right – have a sandwich, my dear,' he said to Daisy.

Daisy took a sandwich and began to nibble it very daintily.

'What about you?' said the pageboy to Mr Horspath. 'Don't you want one?'

'Oh, all right,' said Mr Horspath, to get rid of him. But the boy stayed there, glaring at him fixedly. Mr Horspath began to get nervous.

'Go away,' he said. 'Shoo. Go and feed someone else.'

The boy drifted away, but he didn't take his eyes off Mr Horspath for a moment.

'Ha ha,' said Mr Horspath to Daisy. 'Amusing little rascal.'

'I thought he was sweet,' said Daisy. 'He looked like young Thunderbolt from Clayton Terrace.'

'Daisy,' Mr Horspath murmured, moving a little closer to her, 'I'm glad we're alone. I want to ask you – Yes? Yes? What do you want?'

For another pageboy had appeared, with a plate of sausage rolls. This boy was bigger than the first one, but he was glaring just as intently.

'Sausage roll?' he said, in the same tone of voice as if he'd said, 'D'you want a fight?'

'No, I don't want a sausage roll,' said Mr Horspath irritably. 'Go away.'

'Well, *she* might,' said the boy, and thrust the plate at Daisy.

'Hello, Benny,' she said. 'Fancy seeing you here. Is your Ma and Pa coming?'

'Yeah,' he said. 'Only not in costume. Leah is, though. She's coming as the Queen of Sheba.'

'Oh, lovely! I wish I'd come in costume now. I could have been a Gypsy Maiden.'

'You look very lovely as you are,' said Mr Horspath gallantly, trying to get between Benny and Daisy. 'Go away, boy. When we want a sausage roll, we'll ask for it.'

Benny glared at him through narrowed eyes, and retreated. Mr Horspath turned back to Daisy.

'Daisy,' he murmered softly. 'May I have the next dance? To waltz around the floor with you in my arms would be – Yes? Yes? Yes? What is it *this* time?'

'I thought you might have finished your sandwich,' said Thunderbolt. 'I got plenty more here.'

'Go away! Go away!'

'There's cucumber in them triangular ones, and the other ones is a sort of fishpaste, I think. I just opened one up to have a look.'

'We don't want – '

'They don't smell of anything in pertickler. I smelt 'em too. I suppose it could be jam.'

This boy was driving him to the point of madness,

Mr Horspath felt. And then he looked up and saw Daisy waltzing away with a gondolier.

'*Hnnhmhnnhmmm*,' was the way Thunderbolt would have spelled the sound that came from between Mr Horspath's gritted teeth. Thunderbolt thought it best to move away.

Meanwhile, out by the cloakroom, Angela and Zerlina were talking to Dick, who had just arrived.

He was looking as bandit-like as the New Cut Gang could make him. He wore a black cloak made out of a curtain, two wide leather belts over his shoulders and across his chest for bandoliers, and knee-length riding boots they'd borrowed from the stable. Most of his face was hidden behind a black mask across his eyes and a ferocious black beard made of horsehair and dyed with ink.

'I'm not very comfortable in this get-up,' he whispered to Angela. 'The blooming mask keeps getting in me way. You ain't cut the holes big enough. And the beard's awful scratchy, and these boots is crippling me. Is Daisy here yet?'

'Yeah,' said Zerlina. 'She's dancing with Alf.'

'Oh, Alf, eh,' said Dick, his eyes glittering dangerously behind the mask.

'You don't want to worry about him,' said Angela. 'It's old Horspath what's the real danger. Here, go on, hurry up and get in the ballroom – we got more guests coming in.'

They shoved Dick through the door and into the ballroom, which was now getting crowded. The Major-Domo at the door, who was announcing all the guests as they arrived, asked him for his name.

Dick blinked in alarm, and had to shove the mask back into position.

'Oh – er – my name – yeah – er – Mr Scampolati,' he said hastily. 'From Sicily.'

'Mr Scampolati,' said the Major-Domo loudly. 'From Sicily.'

No one took any notice, so Dick moved into the big room and looked around. As well as Alf the gondolier and Giuseppe the cow-puncher there were eight Demon Kings, three Mad Monks, four Pirates, one Henry the Eighth, one Arab Chieftain, and at least half a dozen men dressed as policemen. Dick found himself standing next to one of them in a crowded corner between dances, and nodded in a friendly way. The policeman nodded back.

'Nice costume, mate,' said Dick.

'This ain't a costume,' said the policeman. 'I'm on duty.'

Dick uttered a strangled whinny.

'You all right?' said the policeman.

'Yeah. I must of swallowed a fly,' mumbled Dick. 'You – er – chasing anyone, then?'

'In a manner of speaking,' said the policeman mysteriously. 'We got word as how the perpetrator of the Gas-Fitters' Hall burglary is likely to be here tonight to make a daring raid on all the ladies' jewels.'

'No, really?'

'Yeah. Seems like it's that feller as broke out of prison last night. A desperate character, by all accounts.'

Dick was speechless.

'Keep your eyes open, eh?' said the policeman,

and tapped his nose significantly before moving away.

Blimey, thought Dick, this is awful. The place is crawling with rozzers! He looked around and seemed to see them everywhere, like beetles.

So when he felt a soft hand on his arm he jumped a foot and let out a yelp of fear.

'Dick!' said Daisy. 'It's only me.'

'Heck,' he muttered. 'Daisy! Blimey. Lawks! Come behind this aspidistra . . .'

He led her behind the nearest plant, and from the dark green shadow of the leaves he peered out at the brightly lit dance-floor, where couples were twirling about to the music of 'The Gasworks Polka'.

'Dick!' she said. 'What's the matter?'

'I'm on the run, Daisy!' he said. 'I'm a wanted man. The place is full of coppers all looking for me.'

'I know!' she said, and her eyes glowed with admiration. 'It's ever so daring of you. I think you're wonderful, Dick!'

'Do you?' he said. 'Cor. The thing is, they think I done the burglary.'

'They never!'

'They do. I was just talking to one of 'em. If they catch me, I could get ten years, easy. Probably twenty. Here, d'you like my costume, Daisy?'

'Not half,' she said. 'It suits you marvellous. You look ever so handsome! I can't hardly see your face at all.'

Dick wondered if this was the right moment to propose, but before he could clear his throat and blush and shuffle his feet and begin, there was a rustle, and the leaves of the aspidistra parted.

'Ah, there you are, Daisy!' said the smooth voice of Mr Horspath. 'Naughty, naughty girl! Hiding away from me! Come and dance. You know you promised!'

Dick growled, and Mr Horspath wagged a finger at him.

'Come, come!' he said. 'You mustn't hide the loveliest girl at the ball away like this! Give the other fellows a chance, ha ha!'

Dick frowned as fiercely as he could, but unluckily this displaced the mask, and he found he couldn't see anything at all. Without thinking he put up his hand to adjust it.

Mr Horspath gasped.

'Wait a minute!' he said, and struck an attitude of horror. 'I know that face! That's Smith, isn't it? You're the scoundrel that – Help! Police! Help! Over here!'

In a fury, Dick tore off his scratchy beard and aimed a punch at Mr Horspath's nose. But it didn't connect, because a burly constable seized his arm. In a second whistles were blowing, heavy boots were thundering across the dance-floor, and Dangerous Dick Smith, the Lambeth Bandit, was firmly in the hands of the law.

'Is this him, Inspector?' said the Sergeant.

The music had stopped; all the dancers had spread out in a ring around the group by the aspidistra – Mr Horspath pointing dramatically, Daisy with her hands to her cheeks in despair, and two great big policemen holding a struggling, snarling Dick.

The Inspector stepped up and took off Dick's mask.

'Yes,' he said. 'This is him. This is our man. Well done, Mr Horspath, sir!'

And close to the bandstand, Benny and Thunderbolt looked at each other in dismay. This wasn't what they'd planned at all.

But the twins hadn't been fooling when they spoke about a big surprise. Having bagged the Archbishop of Canterbury before, they'd got ambitious, and gone for even bigger game this time – and got it. For suddenly there came a bang on the floor from the Major-Domo's mace, and the doors were flung wide, and the Major-Domo bellowed:

'Ladies and gentlemen! His Royal Highness The Prince of Wales!'

Seven

The Left-luggage Ticket

The Prince of Wales was a stout middle-aged gentleman wearing evening dress, with a grey beard and a cigar. He was accompanied by half a dozen grandlooking lords and ladies and swells all covered in medals and ribbons and ostrich feathers and monocles and diamond studs. And on either side of the Prince, looking triumphant, came Angela and Zerlina.

The appearance of the Royal party caused a sensation. Ladies curtseyed, gentlemen bowed, and the Light Bombardiers played 'God Save the Queen'.

Benny nudged Thunderbolt.

'See?' he whispered. 'Never bet against the twins. They're blooming supernatural, they are.'

'But what are we going to do about – '

'Ssh! Wait.'

And Benny put his finger to his lips, because the Prince of Wales had put down his cigar and was looking around genially.

'Thank you for your kind reception,' said the Prince to everyone in general. 'These two young ladies came to see my Private Secretary this morning and told us all about the Ball, and we couldn't resist. But what's going on here? Are you playing charades?'

Everyone was too shy to answer. With an effort Inspector Gorman of the Yard swallowed his amazement and said, 'Er – no, Your Royal Highness, sir. We just apprehended this villain in the act of committing assault and battery, sir. He escaped from prison last night, sir.'

'Bless my soul,' said the Prince of Wales. 'And I hear you had a burglary here? Frightful bad luck. Lose a lot?'

The Worshipful Master of the Gas-Fitters' Company stepped forward and bowed.

'All our silver, Your Royal Highness. Over ten thousand pounds' worth of irreplaceable antiques.'

'Good Lord,' said the Prince. 'Caught the burglars yet, Inspector?'

'Well, Your Royal Highness – '

And at this point Mr Horspath seemed to ooze his way forward. Without actually stepping there, he appeared beside the Inspector and bowed very deeply to the Prince of Wales.

'Albert Horspath,' he said in reverential tones. 'Deputy Gasworks Manager. If I may make an announcement, Your Royal Highness, we might get to the bottom of the mystery sooner than we had hoped.'

There was a ripple of excitement around the ballroom. Everyone was listening now; the waiters and the cooks and the musicians as well as all the guests were gaping open-mouthed at what was going on. It was as good as a play.

'Jolly good,' said the Prince. 'Carry on.'

'Thank you, sir,' said Mr Horspath, making a squirmy sort of bow. 'The fact is, I had not till this minute made the connection in my mind between what I saw the other night and the burglary itself. It was only seeing this rogue Smith here dressed in this suspicious way that reminded me.'

'You're a wavy-haired weasel!' shouted Dick.

'You keep quiet,' said the Inspector. 'Carry on, Mr Horspath.'

'The other night,' said Mr Horspath, 'the night of the burglary, that is to say, I was taking my evening stroll when I saw this man climbing the fire-escape at the side of the building here.'

'You never did!' shouted Dick. 'You oily-eyed poodle-faker!'

'You hold your noise,' thundered the Inspector. 'None of that forceful language! Don't you know who you're a-speaking in front of?'

Dick shut his mouth mutinously, and Mr Horspath, looking pious and sorrowful, went on:

'Yes, I saw him climbing the fire-escape with a sack on his back. Knowing that Mr Whittle keeps a pigeon-loft up there, I naturally assumed that he had employed Smith to look after his pigeons, and that Smith was carrying bird-seed or something of the sort. All we have to do is look, Inspector.'

Thunderbolt gasped at the wickedness of the man, but Benny whispered, 'Ssh! Wait! We ain't got him yet. Not quite.'

The Prince of Wales turned to the Inspector.

'Sounds a simple enough suggestion, Inspector. Why don't you send a constable up to have a look round?'

'Off you go, Hopkins!' said the Inspector, and a brisk-looking constable saluted smartly and ran off towards the stairs.

While they waited for him to come back, the

guests whispered in excitement. Thunderbolt saw Mr Whittle looking very disturbed, and Miss Honoria holding his arm tightly.

Then they heard the constable's footsteps coming back at the double. He ran in, panting, saluted again, and said, 'Nothing there, sir. Just pigeons.'

There was a sigh of disappointment from everyone, but Benny was watching Mr Horspath. He saw him gulp and flick his eyes around swiftly before recovering himself.

'Obviously the rogue managed to move his ill-gotten booty away,' Mr Horspath said. 'You only have to interrogate him, Inspector.'

'I never done no such thing, you soapy serpent!' shouted Dick.

Benny took a deep breath and muttered to Thunderbolt, 'Here goes.'

Then he stepped forward.

Everyone's eyes turned to him, including the heavy-lidded ones belonging to the Prince of Wales. Benny felt the thrill of stardom.

'I know where it is,' he said.

There was a gasp from everyone, and the biggest one of all came from Mr Horspath.

'Oh, good evening, Your Royal Highness, sir,' Benny went on politely, because out of the corner of his eye he saw his father and mother gazing at him horrified, and thought he'd better be on his best behaviour.

'And who are you?' said the Prince.

'Benny Kaminsky, Your Royal Highness. I'm a detective,' Benny explained. 'And yesterday I was doing some detecting and I happened to detect Mr

Whittle going up to his pigeon-loft. I was in disguise so he probly don't know it was me.'

Everyone looked at Mr Whittle, and then back to Benny.

'Anyway, when I was there I detected that the Gas-Fitters' Hall silver *was* there, just like Mr Horspath said. I saw it behind the sacks of bird-seed.'

Mr Whittle's eyes had narrowed. As for Mr Horspath, he had gone very pale. But he nodded and said, 'I thought so. The boy's right. Oh, yes.'

And the policeman said, 'It weren't there a minute ago, sir. I looked everywhere.'

'No,' said Benny, 'cause me and Thunderbolt moved it.'

Everyone gasped. Thunderbolt stepped forward and bowed very low to the Prince of Wales.

'This is Thunderbolt Dobney, Your Royal Highness,' said Benny. 'Me and him went up there last night and moved all the silver away to a place of safety, cause we reckoned that someone was trying to put the blame on someone else. We reckoned they was trying to put the blame on Mr Whittle, and we knew that Mr Whittle wouldn't nick the silver, cause that's ridiculous.'

'Thank you very much, Benny,' said Mr Whittle.

'So where is it?' said Inspector Gorman. 'What'd you do with it?'

Benny fished in his pocket and pulled out a crumpled scrap of paper.

'It's in the left-luggage office at Waterloo Station,' he said. 'Here's the ticket.'

'Cor!' said the twins at the same moment, in deep admiration.

The Inspector took the ticket and gave it to the Sergeant.

'Take a couple of men and nip round there quick,' he said. 'It's only five minutes away.'

The Sergeant and two constables hurried away. The Inspector turned back to Benny, looking fierce.

'Do you know that you have committed a grave offence?' he thundered. 'You oughter come and told the police immediately, instead of concealing the evidence! You could be severely punished for this!'

'Yeah, but if we done that,' said Thunderbolt, 'well, if we done that you'd never have found out who done the burglary.'

'And how are we going to find that out anyway?'

'It's obvious,' said Benny. 'The only person what knew the silver was there was the one as put it there in the first place. Mr Horspath, of course!'

Mr Horspath gave a ghastly grin, and then a merry laugh.

'Ha, ha!' he said. 'Jolly good yarn, Benny! Amusing, isn't it, sir?' he said to the Prince of Wales. 'I knew it was there because I saw that rotter Smith taking it up there, as I told you before, Inspector,' he added.

'We thought you'd say that,' said Benny. 'So we got someone else to come along. Your Royal Highness, may I present the famous escaped prisoner Sid the Swede?'

The Arab Chieftain stepped forward, lifting the robe to avoid falling over again. He took off the head-dress, and there was Sid the Swede.

'Benny told me as I'd probly get off if I told the truth,' he said shakily. 'I hope he's right, Your Majesty.'

The Prince of Wales raised his eyebrows.

'We'll see about that,' said Inspector Gorman. 'Well, Sid? What's your part in this affair?'

'Well, sir,' said Sid, twisting his fingers together, 'about a fortnight ago, sir, that gentleman come to me with a hoffer.'

He pointed to Mr Horspath.

'With a what?' said the Prince.

'With a hoffer of hemployment, sir. He had a little job for me. He give me a few shillings and he hasked me to purchase a sack for him, sir.'

'Ha, ha, ha!' laughed Mr Horspath. 'Jolly good joke! Ha ha!'

'Why didn't he buy it hisself?' said the Inspector.

'I think he didn't want it generally known as he was in the market for sacks, Your Honour. Anyway, I took the money, and then I fell into temptation, sir.'

'Temptation?' said the Prince.

'I'm afraid so, sir. Snake-Eyes – I mean, Mr Melmott was hoffering some very generous hodds in a sporting matter, and I laid it all on young D – I mean on the orse of my choice, sir. So once I'd done that, I had no money left and no sack neither, sir. So you see the dilemma what I was in, Your Royal Ighness.'

'Very tricky indeed,' said the Prince. 'So what did you do?'

'I done what any man would have done in the circumstances, Your Royal Ighness. I raided a washing line.'

'Yes, yer did, didn't yer!' came a voice from the crowd, and the people nearby turned to look at the stout and purple form of Mrs Liza Pearson. When she realized that everyone was looking at her, including the Prince of Wales, she became even purpler, and curtseyed. 'Begging your pardon, Your Royal Highness, but I saw this sneaking snivelling scoundrel making off with my washing. I couldn't give chase at the time, being up to me elbows in suds, but I caught im later round the Dog and Duck and gave im in charge. They oughter sent im down for ten year at least!'

'What did he steal?' said the Prince.

'He stole a pillow-case, Your Royal Highness!' she said, quivering with indignation.

'Yes, I did, sir, I admit it,' said Sid the Swede, nodding rapidly. 'And I give it to *im* instead of the sack as he wanted me to get.'

He pointed to Mr Horspath, who laughed heartily.

'Oh, this is rich!' Mr Horspath said. 'What a yarn, sir! Ha ha ha!'

'Yes, indeed,' said the Prince of Wales. 'I'm enjoying it immensely. And I think I can hear your men coming back, Inspector. I wonder what they've found.'

And everyone turned to the ballroom doors. No great star of the theatre or the music hall had ever had a more dramatic entrance than the Sergeant and the two constables. They came puffing in carrying a great big canvas sack marked JOBSON'S HORSE NUTS and put it down with a clank.

'But you see,' cried Mr Horspath, 'that's a sack! An ordinary sack!'

'Well, course it is,' said Benny. 'We couldn't leave it in the left-luggage office in just a pillow-case, could we?'

'Open it up, Sergeant,' said the Inspector.

The Sergeant stopped mopping his brow and untied the length of hairy string around the neck of the sack. Benny knew what was in it, of course, so he couldn't resist looking at the effect it was all having on the guests. He'd never seen such wide eyes in his life – hundreds of them, all peering at the sack. It was marvellous.

'Here it is, Inspector!' said the Sergeant, and pulled out a dirty white bag, and from the bag took out a gleaming silver gas-worker's wrench on an ebony plinth.

'The silver!' cried the Worshipful Master. 'The Jabez Calcutt Memorial Trophy!'

'My pillow-case!' cried Mrs Liza Pearson.

More and more silver was coming out of the pillow-case: great big dishes, cups, goblets, trays, salt-cellars. It gleamed and shone and glittered, and the only person who wasn't delighted was Mr Horspath.

He was looking ghastly pale. A fearful sweat stood out on his forehead, and his wavy hair hung in limp strands over his ears. But he still had enough presence of mind to laugh.

'Ha, ha! Jolly good jape! I hope you're going to put that young rascal away for a long time, Inspector. Slandering my reputation is a serious matter. I shall be consulting my lawyers in the morning.'

The Prince of Wales was never happy for long without a cigar in his hand, and having put his last one down more than twenty minutes ago, he was impatient for another. As he lifted it to his lips Mr Horspath darted to his side, matchbox in hand, and struck a light for him.

'Here you are, sir! Allow me!' he said.

And as soon as he'd lit the cigar, Benny darted to him and snatched the matchbox away.

'What are you doing?' said Mr Horspath. 'Look at him, Inspector! A common little sneak-thief! He can't leave anything alone!'

But Benny wasn't listening. He was intent on fishing a screw of paper out of his pocket, and taking out a match, and comparing the length of it with Mr Horspath's.

'That's it!' he cried in triumph. 'We got him! This is the final proof!'

And he danced around like a mad thing.

The Prince of Wales puffed at his cigar and said, 'When you've finished dancing, would you mind explaining, young man?'

'We found this dead lucifer under the window in the alley where he got in! And it's a Swedish one, and they're longer'n English matches! And *he's* been to Sweden, and the one he's just lit the cigar with is the same! It's him, and we proved it!'

And that was too much for Mr Horspath. Seeing himself finally trapped, he gave a wild cry and rushed for the thinnest part of the crowd, meaning to escape.

But unluckily for him, the thinnest part of the crowd was where Henry the Eighth was standing, and as Mr Horspath tried to dodge past, the famous king reached out a mighty hand and grabbed him. Mr Horspath wriggled like a maggot, he squealed like a pig, but he was caught.

'Where d'you think you're going?' said Henry the Eighth, and the twins cried, 'Orlando!'

'Yus, it's me,' said Orlando. 'Here you are, Inspector, take your prisoner.'

The policemen put some handcuffs on Mr Horspath, who snarled villainously.

'Well, this seems to have ended very happily,' said the Prince of Wales. 'May I congratulate the young detectives?'

He shook hands with Benny and Thunderbolt.

'Er – ' said Sid the Swede. 'I was just wondering, you know –'

'Yeah, what about Sid?' said Benny. 'He come here at the risk of more imprisonment so's he could help catch Mr Horspath, didn't he? So you oughter let him go!'

'Ah, but he broke out of prison,' said the Inspector. 'So did young Dick here. That's a serious matter on its own.'

And Orlando stepped forward in his Henry the Eighth costume and bowed to the Prince.

'I have a confession to make,' he said. 'It was me what helped 'em break out. My name is Orlando, Your Royal Highness, perfessional strong man. I climbed up a ladder and I got hold the bars like *that* – and I wrenched 'em like *that* – and I heaved and I twisted like *that* – till there was room for 'em to get out. So part of the blame is mine, Your Royal Highness. And if there's the handcuffs what can hold me, I shall be honoured to put my hands in 'em.'

Angela looked at Zerlina, and Zerlina looked at Angela.

'Well,' said Angela, 'really . . .'

'It was our idea all the time,' said Zerlina.

'And we nicked the ladder out of Charlie Ladysmith's yard . . .'

'And we woke Orlando up by throwing stones at him.'

'Oh, I'm used to that,' said Orlando, in case anyone thought the twins had been cruel. 'You seen the act, Your Royal Highness? The best bit is where they bounce cannon-balls off me head. I'll send you a ticket. I reckon I oughter pay me debt to society now. But,' he said dramatically, 'before I go inside, I got an announcement to make.'

He took off the Henry the Eighth hat and beard and looked properly like Orlando again, and then he said:

'Some time ago I fell in love with a young lady. I done everything I could to please her, like crushing rocks and eating yards of anchor-chain, but I never had the nerve to do what I really wanted to do and propose to her. And seeing as she's here tonight, I'd like to do it here and now afore I lose me nerve.'

And he got to one knee and held out his hands to Miss Honoria Whittle.

'Honoria, will you be my wife?' he said. 'Will you share the rough-and-ready life of a perfessional strong man?'

'Oh, Orlando! Of course I will!'

And the band, who'd been following everything, played a loud chord of C Major as the two of them embraced.

Thunderbolt was amazed.

'So *he's* the one with the love phoby!' he said. 'Miss Whittle said she knew someone else with one – just like Dick!'

And that reminded everyone of Dick, who stood there still under police guard, together with Sid the Swede, who'd been re-arrested.

Then Benny had an inspiration.

'Excuse me, Your Royal Highness,' he said. 'Seeing as we've detected the real burgular, and seeing as we couldn't of done it without Sid the Swede, and seeing as Dick was only inside for clocking Mr Horspath one on the razzo when he made up to Daisy behind the potted palm, what about a Royal Pardon?'

The Prince of Wales considered it, puffing at his cigar and eyeing Benny thoughtfully.

'Properly speaking, you ought to apply to Her Majesty the Queen,' he said. 'But in the circumstances I am sure she would agree to your request. Release them, Inspector!'

And the police unlocked the handcuffs. Sid the Swede slunk away to avoid Mrs Pearson, and Dick stood blinking with embarrassment in the centre of a cheering circle of friends and neighbours, clapping him on the back and shaking his hand.

Then someone said, 'Go on, Dick! Ask her!'

And someone else yelled, 'Here she is! Go it, Dick!'

And there was Daisy, looking bashful. Everyone was looking on and grinning, including the policemen, because some of them had had a quiet bet with Snake-Eyes Melmott, too. The only one who didn't know what it was all about was the Prince of Wales, but Angela plucked his sleeve and whispered to him, and he smiled.

And Dick stood there getting redder and redder. He looked down at the floor; he looked up at the ceiling. He opened his mouth – he closed it again.

He looked around for escape, just as Mr Horspath had done.

'Oh no,' whispered Thunderbolt. 'He's not gonna do it . . .'

Then the Prince of Wales bent and whispered something to Zerlina, who scampered around and plucked at the sleeve of the band-leader and whispered something to *him*; and the band-leader said something to the band, and they raised their instruments, took a deep breath, and began to play.

And everyone recognized the tune, and laughed and joined in:

> 'Daisy, Daisy, give me your answer, do!
> I'm half crazy, all for the love of you;
> It won't be a stylish marriage -
> I can't afford a carriage;
> But you'll look sweet, upon the seat
> Of a bicycle made for two!'

And the loudest singing of all came from Dick, and by the time the song was over, somehow he had proposed, and somehow she had accepted, and they stood there blushing like two tomatoes and looking very happy.

'Well, my congratulations to the happy couples,' said the Prince of Wales.

And he shook hands with Dick, and with Daisy and Miss Whittle, who both curtseyed. And then he held out his hand to Orlando.

'Ah,' said Orlando. 'Now I'd like to shake your hand, sir, but I daren't. You see, this hand of mine can crush rocks.'

'You crush rocks with your hand?' said the Prince. 'I bet you can't.'

'Did I hear you say *bet*, Your Royal Highness?' said a rich and fruity voice. 'May I offer my services?'

'Snake-Eyes Melmott!' said Angela.

The famous bookmaker had appeared as if by magic, with his little black book in hand.

'I can offer odds in the matter of rock-crushing to any lady or gentleman present,' he said, and within a minute he was doing a brisk trade. The Prince of Wales bet ten guineas that Orlando couldn't, and Mr Whittle bet ten guineas that he could, and dozens of other bets were entered in the little black book. Angela and Zerlina were watching closely. It turned out that more people thought Orlando couldn't than thought he could, so if he could, Snake-Eyes Melmott would win. And since he hardly ever lost, that would have been the way to bet – if the gang had had any money to bet with.

'I wish he'd paid out on the other bet first,' said Thunderbolt. 'Then I could've put all me winnings on Orlando and won a *fortune*.'

When all the bets were laid, a space was cleared in the centre of the dance-floor, and a servant came in with a silver tray covered in a snowy white napkin, in the middle of which was a rock the size of an orange.

'Right,' said Orlando. 'Now you better all stand back a bit, on account of flying chips of rock.'

Miss Whittle kissed him for luck, and he rolled up his sleeves to reveal the biggest muscles anyone had ever seen. He took the rock in his right hand, weighing it carefully. From the band came a low roll on the snare drum.

Orlando raised the rock high. The drumbeat got louder.

He gritted his teeth. The veins stood out on his head. He began to squeeze. The muscles in his arm bulged even bigger. The drumbeat got louder still.

And then the rock began to crumble. A trail of powder fell to the floor, and suddenly there was nothing in Orlando's hand but bits of gravel and sand. There was a crash from the cymbals, an even louder chord of C major from the band, and everyone cheered and clapped, including the Prince of Wales.

Orlando brushed his hands together and bowed. The gang watched Snake-Eyes Melmott paying out to those who'd won.

'H'mm,' said Benny. 'Well, at least we'll get our winnings from the main bet.'

And while most of the guests were dancing or eating or drinking toasts to the newly engaged couples, a line of eager punters was forming at one side of the ballroom to get their money from Snake-Eyes Melmott. Everyone who'd put money on Dick was there, from Sid the Swede to the local Vicar.

Thunderbolt could hardly contain his excitement. All that money! And beating Snake-Eyes Melmott!

But it seemed as if there was a problem. Thunderbolt stopped grinning and listened.

'Ladies and gentlemen,' Snake-Eyes was saying, 'may I introduce the well-known and highly respected timekeeper, Mr Bell, known to members of the boxing fraternity as Ding-Dong. Ding-Dong Bell's timekeeping is known to be immaculate, which is why I invited him along this evening to make a careful note of the proceedings in case there was any dispute about the finish. Mr Bell.'

Ding-Dong Bell was a thin, scholarly-looking man with no less than three different kinds of watch. He placed them all on the table in front of him.

'Them watches,' he said, 'was synchronized by me personal, to the chimes of Big Ben, at six o'clock last. And according to them, young Dick's proposal, as noted by two independent witnesses, took place at five minutes past midnight.'

'Well, ladies and gentlemen,' said Snake-Eyes Melmott, 'what a shame, what a shame! You all remember the terms of the bet: Dick had to propose and be accepted before twelve o'clock. So I'm afraid you all lost. However, the good news is I'm opening a book on the likelihood of living dinosaurs being discovered in the South American jungle by the Royal Geographical Expedition. I can offer you a hundred to one against a pterodactyl – how's that? Can't say fairer than that. Hundred to one, gents! Any takers?'

With cries of disappointment and dismay the people turned away, tearing up their betting slips and shaking their heads at their own folly.

'We should of known,' said Angela darkly.

'I could of sworn we had him this time!' said Zerlina.

'We'll get him yet. He's not beating us like that . . .'

Thunderbolt and Benny looked at each other. Their disgust was almost too deep for words.

'Cor,' said Benny finally. 'I mean to say, well, *blimey*.'

Thunderbolt couldn't say anything. The future

was clear to him: gambling, drink, loose women, ruin, prison, the gallows. If only he'd paid more attention to 'The Primrose Path, or If Only He Had Known'!

He gulped. It was going to be very hard to tell Miss Whittle that he couldn't pay her; never mind telling Pa . . .

There was a slight cough, and they looked around. Mr Whittle stood there, with the Worshipful Master of the Ancient and Worshipful Company of Gas-Fitters.

'Young gents,' said the Worshipful Master, 'and young ladies too, I understand. Commendable ingenuity and initiative. Daring and resourceful plan. On behalf of the Ancient and Worshipful Company of Gas-Fitters, I should be proud to offer you a reward of ten pounds each, and invite you all to partake of ice-cream with His Royal Highness the Prince of Wales. If you would care to step this way . . .'

And everything was all right, just like that.

So the New Cut Gang sat down with the Prince of Wales, and watched Orlando dancing with Miss Whittle, and Dick dancing with Daisy, and the silver gleaming on the sideboard, and Mr Miller showing three young men how to keep themselves cool by the application of cucumber, and everyone having a whale of a time.

'I think this is probably the social event of the Season,' said the Prince of Wales. 'Thank you for inviting me to the Gas-Fitters' Ball.'

'It was a pleasure,' said Angela. 'By the way . . .'

'I don't suppose you know where we can get a pterodactyl?' said Zerlina.